ARE YOU SCARED YET?

Haunted Houses

ARE YOU SCARED YET?

Houses

ROBERT D. SAN SOUCI

Illustrated by **KELLY MURPHY**

& ANTOINE REVOY

SQUARE
FISH

HENRY HOLT AND COMPANY ∽ NEW YORK

SQUARE FISH

An Imprint of Macmillan

Library of Congress Cataloging-in-Publication Data
San Souci, Robert D.
Haunted houses / Robert D. San Souci ; illustrated by Kelly Murphy and
Antoine Revoy.
p.   cm. — (Are you scared yet?)
"Christy Ottaviano Books."
Contents: Chimera House — Webs — Dollhouse — Tea house —
Dust creatures — Many — The lodge — La Casa de las Muertas —
Doghouse — The haunted mansion.
ISBN 978-0-312-55136-0
1. Haunted houses—Juvenile fiction.   2. Horror tales, American.
3. Children's stories, American.   [1. Haunted houses—Fiction.
2. Horror stories.   3. Short stories.]   I. Murphy, Kelly, ill.
II. Revoy, Antoine, ill.   III. Title.
PZ7.S1947Hau 2010   [Fic]—dc22   2009050763

Originally published in the United States by
Christy Ottaviano Books/Henry Holt and Company
First Square Fish Edition: July 2012
Square Fish logo designed by Filomena Tuosto
Book designed by April Ward
mackids.com

1 3 5 7 9 10 8 6 4 2

AR: 6.1 / LEXILE: 900L

To Dirk Alphin,
whose help on this volume—
and countless others—
has been immeasurable

—R. S. S.

CONTENTS

ARE YOU SCARED YET?

Haunted Houses

Chimera House

"It is *the* scariest place *ever*," said Demond.

His girlfriend, Rachelle, sitting next to him, just rolled her eyes.

"Uh-huh," Demetrius, his brother, called Little D, responded—being cool, not playing along. He was angry, stuck in between Antoine and Lorelle—both of them hefty. For all they played at being in love, they didn't want to middle-seat it where a metal bar made riding a real pain. This was especially true when Demond, the world's worst driver in Little D's mind, hit a pothole or bump at full speed. Then the boy felt like he was getting mashed between two rolled mattresses. Every part of this trip seemed stupid.

Demond, put off by his little brother's attitude, continued. "It's five stories high—each floor scarier than the last one. You get your money back if you get through floor five."

"How much does it cost?" asked Antoine.

"Twenty-five."

Antoine whistled. "That's scary enough! But it's got a money-back guarantee, you said."

Demond hawked out a laugh. "They say it's so scary no one ever got all the way through."

"What, afraid of plastic skeletons and cardboard monsters and glow-in-the-dark ghosts?"

"It's much scarier than that," Demond insisted.

"How do you know so much?" challenged Little D. "You been there?"

"No—ain't that many people ever been there. You got to know somebody."

"So who do *you* know?" asked Rachelle. "You never told me."

"Toussaint. Couple of weeks ago, we were taking care of a little business. And I got to asking him about that voo-doo stuff he messes with. Then we got to talking about other scary stuff. I asked him if he'd ever seen a ghost. Yeah, he said, and plenty of other things. That's when he told me about this place. He said it's scary as all get-out—and it might really be haunted, too."

Before Rachelle could say anything, Lorelle piped up.

"*Toussaint!*" Lorelle made no effort to hide the disgust in her voice. "That is one crazy dude. We're on a wild-goose chase, for sure."

"Wild *ghost* chase, you mean," said Antoine, cracking up at his own joke. Lorelle just grunted, folded her arms, and stared out the window. But Little D heard her mutter, "This is going to be one big waste of time."

"Funny. I ain't seen Toussaint for almost a week," said Rachelle.

"Toussaint, he always turns up sometime," Demond said.

Little D knew that was wrong. Toussaint had crossed Jamal Machado, a bad man to cross. Unknown to Demond, Little D had begun working for Jamal as a watcher on street corners, using his cell to alert Jamal if he spotted a police car in the area where Jamal was conducting his illegal business. The man, knowing the friendship between Little D's brother and Toussaint, had paid the boy extra to lure Toussaint into a back alley. Jamal had said he and a few of his bros were only going to give Toussaint a warning. But Little D suspected more was at stake. Long after Jamal and his pals had left, he went back into the alley. Toussaint's motionless hand was outflung, his gold-ringed fingers and thumb clenched like a claw. The boy began to run, putting as much distance as fast as he could between himself and what he was responsible for.

No, Toussaint wouldn't turn up ever again.

They were on the road that led northwest out of Detroit toward the suburb of Garriott, some thirty-five miles from town. Newish, gated housing developments and strip malls alternated with lightly wooded patches and meadows. To Little D, who rarely got outside of the city, it was like a different world, afloat in money. It was completely unlike the inner-city world he knew, where the only real possibilities were fast riches through criminal activity or a quick end when caught in the crossfire of a gangland turf war or a police standoff.

As for his brother's legendary haunted house, Little D was inclined to agree with Antoine's opinion that it was "a wild ghost chase." Toussaint—full name Jean Marcelle Toussaint—was anything and everything in the 'hood—number runner, fence, boo and dabbler in darker areas. Folks said he knew voodoo and other secrets from his native Haiti. So just maybe, Little D thought, the guy had some skinny on this scariest place of all. Then he dismissed the idea. No so-called haunted house could be much scarier than the haunted houses that popped up all over Detroit at this time of the year, offering nothing more frightening than bats on strings and face-painted teenagers holding flashlights under their chins or a plateful of soggy spaghetti they called "brains."

Well, it might be worth a laugh—if the place existed. And Demond was paying the way for him and Rachelle. These past weeks, Demond seemed to have a lot of extra cash to throw around. Little D knew better than to ask where it came from, but he was wise enough to take advantage of his brother's sudden generous streak. Neither the money nor the impulse to share would last long with Demond.

"Garriott, next three exits," Rachelle reported. No one else had noticed the road sign.

Keeping his left hand on the wheel, Demond fished a folded paper from the dashboard with his right, unfolded it, and held it so he could read it in the dashboard glow. After studying a moment, he announced, "We want the exit for Montrose Avenue, East."

They quickly passed the first two exits, before Rachelle spotted theirs. Once they were on Montrose, Demond checked his notes again. "Look for Crane Hill Road on the left."

The twisting pavement cut deep into a woodsy area. The route was moonlit, easy enough to follow, but there seemed to be fewer and fewer lights indicating houses.

Little D, used to twenty-four-hour shops, streetlights, and city glow that screened out the stars and softened the night, found the thickening darkness unnerving. Then he spotted the tilted street sign even Rachelle had missed.

"Crane Hill Road!" he shouted so suddenly Demond slammed on the brakes, pitching them all forward against their seat belts—except Antoine, who refused to wear his and slammed against the driver's seat. He cursed loudly, then put his finger to his lip and pulled it away bloody.

"Made me cut myself." His usually good mood was gone. "Look how you're drivin'," he snarled at Demond.

"Wear your seat belt like you're s'posed to," Lorelle said. She sounded pretty put out at this point.

Antoine's rude response left his girlfriend in an angry silence. Now Demetrius felt caught between two sources of anger so electric he could almost feel the bad energy crackling between them. It seemed the evening was going from bad to worse. Everyone was on a short fuse.

Demond waited for two oncoming cars to race past—the first cars they'd seen in a while, Little D realized—then swung onto Crane Hill Road.

It was a single-lane road, walled on both sides by lanky trees and rampant shrubbery that stretched back into thick shadow.

Demond instinctively slowed the car.

"This the road we want?" asked Lorelle. "Looks more like a cow path no self-respectin' cow would use."

Even as she complained, the car jounced through a pothole. Though Demond was cruising at a slower speed, this caused Antoine (who still refused to buckle up) to hit the ceiling, while the others were merely jerked against their belts.

"Tryin' to kill me?" Antoine complained.

"Maybe that's not such a bad idea," Demond called over his shoulder.

"Second that," said Lorelle.

"Watch out!" warned Rachelle.

Demond slowed so that the next pothole caused only minor bouncing.

The branches overhead had become interlaced, as if the trees were deliberately linking limbs to keep moonlight or starlight from reaching the road. To Little D, peering anxiously over the front seat to watch the road ahead, it seemed they had entered a tunnel that was bored into the heart of darkness. With every passing minute, the boy was more convinced that this adventure was one *very bad* idea.

"Toussaint havin' us on, for sure," grumbled Lorelle.

Nobody argued. But Demond kept the car moving ahead, as if determined to prove he hadn't been played for a fool by Toussaint. Little D had a vision of Toussaint roaring with laughter when he heard about their foolishness. Then he remembered . . . that man wasn't going to laugh ever again.

The road curved this way and that. Little D, looking right, left, straight ahead, his neck in constant motion, imagined flicking shapes and glowing eyes in the shadows surrounding them. The surface was growing bumpier; the woods were pressing closer; it was clearly a mistake to be here. He wondered why Demond was pushing on.

And then, around the next bend, the road ended in a gravel-surfaced parking lot, well lit by floodlights on high, metal poles. A scattering of cars was spread out across the generous parking area. Beyond, towering above the lot and brightly lit gardens, was the floodlit façade of a towering, five-story mansion. Lights bathed the structure in a garish glow and revealed windows galore, as well as many carved surfaces and an array of gargoyles leering down from the peaked eaves. All the windows were sealed—no trace of light came from inside the building.

"See? Toussaint wasn't jivin' after all," said Demond. To Little D, he sounded both relieved and I-knew-it-all-along smug.

He parked the car under the light stanchion near the stone statues at the head of the concrete walk that cut through the gardens to the massive front doors. Each stone guardian had a lion's head, the body of a goat, and the tail of a snake or dragon. A sign beside the path announced simply CHIMERA HOUSE.

"This must be the place," Demond said unnecessarily. "Everybody out."

It was a relief to stretch his legs, Little D realized, and no longer be squashed between the other backseat passengers.

Everyone luxuriated in the fresh air and the chance to stand and move about. Demond put his arm around Rachelle's shoulders, and she snuggled close to him. They started toward the house. Antoine and Lorelle followed separately. Little D could still sense anger between them. He brought up the rear, glad to be out of the car but not quite sure he wanted to explore the secrets—hokey or genuinely scary—inside Chimera House.

At the end of the path, a short flight of broad steps led up to a wide porch, sheltered by a roof supported by tall columns. The high, wooden double doors were carved with strange human figures and inhuman creatures and bunches of grapes, leaves, and flowers. Matching squares of thick, milky glass, about the height of a man's head, revealed some light inside. There was a doorbell below an illuminated sign: HOURS OF OPERATION: WED—SUN, II A.M.—MIDNIGHT.

Demond pushed the bell, and the right-hand door swung open. The five entered single-file. Inside was a vast, circular, marble-floored area. A long wooden counter and waist-high wooden barrier divided it in half. Three people—two men and one woman—were seated behind the counter. The men, off to one side, were deep in conversation over a computer console; they barely glanced up at the visitors before returning their attention to the screen. The woman directly in front of them welcomed them with a smile. Though there was overhead fluorescent lighting, the bright glow from some kind of console recessed in the desk surface lit her face from below, giving her a faintly ghostly look.

Little D wondered if the effect was deliberate, to get folks in the mood for a "fright night."

Still smiling, she took care of the ticket sales.

Antoine, buying the ticket he had apparently promised Lorelle, said, "I understand if I get all the way through this place, I get my money back."

"That is correct," the woman said. To Little D, it seemed her smile grew bigger at the thought of anyone really collecting on this guarantee. He felt a chill. In the weird light, her smile seemed almost wolfish.

"Let's get goin'," said Demond, rubbing his palms together in a great show of enthusiasm.

"Please enter by the gate. I'll buzz you through."

She pushed a button, and a gate in the barrier near her workstation unlatched with a loud click. The five went in.

The woman escorted them to the curved back wall where five closed doors waited.

"There are a few ground rules here at Chimera House. First of all, no more than two persons are to enter at a time." The five glanced at each other. Demond tightened his hold on Rachelle. Antoine and Lorelle, their argument forgotten, took each other's hand.

"Each couple or"—she glanced at Little D—"individual will enter by a different door. But not to worry: You'll all experience everything Chimera House has to offer. Now, then, shall we get on with it? You can spend as much or as little time on a level as you wish. Stairs to the next level are clearly indicated. All levels are closely monitored by security personnel to prevent any—" Here she paused, then gave a look Little D couldn't quite put a name to. "*Problems.* Since we seem to have decided on our divisions, let's go."

She led Demond and Rachelle to the door on the far right. Skipping one door, she ushered Antoine and Lorelle through the middle door. The leftmost door she assigned to Little D. When she opened it, he could see a dimly lit space beyond. He hesitated on the threshold, but she gave him a gentle push between his shoulder blades, and he crossed over.

The first floor was a generous but not very frightening collection of weird things—like a museum of oddities. In jars, in glass display cases, sometimes merely lying in the open on roped-off tables were a two-headed calf, a lamb, and a snake—and, most unsettling, a pair of human Siamese twins floating in what looked like a fish tank filled with some nasty-smelling yellowish fluid. There were a dwarf and a giant human skeleton, both dangling from the ceiling on chains. The sign by the latter indicated the person had been eight feet, three inches tall. There was a display of shrunken heads and a dried human hand with the stubs of candles resting on each of the upturned, claw-like fingers, the "Hand of Glory." It reminded Little D of Toussaint's hand in the alleyway, and he quickly moved on. There was a shriveled-up "Fiji mermaid" that looked like a fake made by sewing together the upper half of a monkey and the tail end of a big fish, then varnishing it to the color of mahogany.

It was ugly, interesting junk as far as Little D was concerned—but nothing more. If this was as bad as it got, he decided, they'd *all* get their money back. The oddest thing was that he didn't see any sign of his companions. He even tried calling his brother's name and each of the others, but there was no response. He had vaguely assumed that all the doors they'd passed through fed into the same area, but now he began to wonder if there were five separate exhibit areas. If so, it would be interesting to find out what the others had seen.

He was growing bored. On a far wall Little D saw a green exit sign. He headed toward it, no longer interested in the contents of the haphazard display cases he passed. Directly below the sign, he found a door opening onto a winding cement staircase leading to the second level. There was nowhere to go but up. *Not much help if there's a fire,* the boy thought. Then he started climbing, taking the stairs two at a time.

The second level proved a bit more interesting. It was set up like a regular Halloween haunted house, and the scares were just about as routine. As soon as Little D stepped out of the stairwell, the lights went out and then the various exhibits began to light up. When he came near one, some kind of motion sensor triggered each gimmick. He did jump a little when an upright coffin suddenly burst open and a mechanical vampire lurched out at him with a shriek. After that he was on his guard against surprises. So the bamboo box that suddenly began to shake while frantic cries came from inside and a claw thrust out from under one corner of the lid didn't startle him. The skeletons dancing around a grave or the ghosts flying by on overhead tracks to recorded screeches—it was all pretty tired and not, in his opinion, likely to scare anyone over the age of eight.

Ignoring the canned sights and sounds, the boy searched for the next exit sign—and found it half hidden by a flock of rubber bats bouncing up and down on cords, their red eyes twinkling on and off.

Because the first two floors failed to produce anything really scary, he started upstairs to level three not really expecting much.

The door to the third floor was closed but unlocked. The knob turned easily, and he pushed his way through. The moment he was inside, the door whooshed shut behind him, and he heard a familiar click. Testing the inner doorknob, he found the door had, indeed, locked itself and wasn't about to budge. He swore loudly, then decided there was nothing to worry about, really: There were surveillance cameras everywhere—and there had to be emergency exits, too. Otherwise, wouldn't Chimera House be breaking the law big time? But then, the police had more important things to do than check on stuff like this, he reasoned. They would probably respond only if there was a big fire and people got trapped.

He glanced around. This looked like more of the first floor: a scattering of display cases, dry fish tanks, and cages that seemed to be made of mesh like the kind on screen doors. Mildly curious, he peered into the nearest glass case—then jumped back with a cry when a big, hairy spider leapt from under a pile of dried leaves on the cage bottom and flattened itself on the glass an inch from his face. Cautiously, he checked out other cages and discovered an assortment of spiders, beetles, snakes, lizards, and so on. On one side, an ugly-looking insect nearly a foot long made a clacking sound with its pincers; across the aisle, giant cockroaches hissed at him. On top of one case full of what looked—and buzzed—like wasps was what appeared to be a huge, stuffed iguana bathed in the warm glow of a metal-shaded bulb. Curious to feel the scaly skin, Little D gave the lifelike creature a poke. To his horror, the thing writhed. It had only been sleeping, basking in the warmth on top of the wasp cage.

Hastily backing away, the boy almost upset the cage with the hissing giant cockroaches. The iguana, probably sluggish from the heat, stretched a claw lazily in the boy's direction, opened its jaws to reveal sharp teeth, then settled back into place, Little D seemingly forgotten.

The boy felt a tickle on his arm. "Gross!" he shouted, batting away the small, spindly-legged spider he discovered

there. He began looking around and quickly realized that there were many creatures outside as well as inside the displays. Spiders and oversized ants and all kinds of bugs crawled across the floor and along the outsides of cages. Overhead, huge moths and black butterflies and other winged things both small and large hovered in clouds over the lit displays.

When a long, green snake glided out from under a table only inches from his foot, Little D knew it was time to make a break for it. The door he'd entered by was locked, so he looked around frantically for another exit and located one across the exhibit floor.

Moving in the direction of the green-lit sign, he followed as direct a path as the jumbled displays would allow. He avoided bumping any of them, even though it sometimes meant moving sideways down particularly narrow aisles, since there seemed to be more and more insects and spiders moving over the glass and mesh surfaces. His progress was slow, because he kept watching his feet to avoid things that slithered or scuttled or crawled through the aisles. He was also busy swatting airborne creatures eager to bite or sting him. Getting angry now, he stomped on several oversize beetles. That made him feel better.

And then, edging around a tall cage filled with bright

red lizards clinging to a lattice of dead twigs, he reached the exit—another closed door.

"Don't let this one be locked," he prayed. But it opened easily enough, the bottom sweeping aside a welter of bugs.

Like the doors earlier, this one closed and latched itself almost instantly. Again, there was nowhere to go but up more cement stairs to the floor above. He realized he was shaking. It ticked him off that a bunch of bugs and lizards and little (surely nonpoisonous) snakes could rattle him this much. Little D was going to be very happy when he collected his money back. Leaving creepy crawlies on the loose was a cheap shot—clearly the owners of Chimera House would pull any trick to turn people back and keep their twenty-five-buck admission fee. Of course, the self-locking doors didn't make much sense, since they didn't allow anyone *to* go back.

Probably some fool forgot to set 'em so they wouldn't lock when folks were passin' through, he told himself. This flight of steps climbed up and up and *up.* By the time he reached the open doorway to level four, he felt winded.

When he caught his breath, he entered a narrow hall-way. The white-painted walls reached up to just below the ceiling, leaving about a foot-and-a-half space between. A short way ahead, the hall became a T, with narrow halls going right and left, quickly becoming Ts themselves.

There was no sign or arrow to indicate which way to go. On a hunch, he turned right, then turned left, holding the vague idea that he was moving away from the stairwell, toward the exit that must lie somewhere ahead. The corridor T'ed again. He took a chance and went left. A short hall, then another T. For no particular reason, he turned right. Two halls opened off either side of this stretch, before he came to another T. Left this time. Two side passages to the left, one to the right. Then another T, again left.

He *thought* he was moving in a generally forward direction, but he wasn't sure anymore. Every passage, every doorway was identical. He understood he was in a maze, the kind those rats ran through in cartoons. But this wasn't funny, since *he* was the rat, trying to find the exit, instead of a hunk of cheese.

Another juncture of three passages. The way ahead was blocked with a one-way gate. Looking right and left, he saw that the other passages were similarly gated.

Sweating, he realized that if he went through a gate, he'd be unable to go back. Somehow, the idea of being forced in any direction worried him. Of course, it was a game, like in a fun house, he assured himself. Nothing could really happen. Still, Little D was uncomfortable. But he didn't want to start shouting for rescue, since that would make him seem weak, and he would not accept that he was weak. If he could cope with the mean streets of the 'hood, he could handle this foolishness, he decided.

Go back and try a different way, he advised himself. But the return seemed far more confusing than pressing forward. He got lost when he couldn't remember if a left turn out was a right turn in. Around and around he went, and finally found himself facing gated ways ahead, right, and left. Or was it the same spot where he'd been before? He was totally lost.

I want out, he admitted, and he pushed through the center gate. Before leaving it behind, he nudged it to assure himself that it was, indeed, a one-way deal. No going back now.

More of the same beyond the gate—*almost*. These passageways were narrower. Little D didn't like tight spaces. But each turn led him into a corridor a fraction narrower than the one he'd left. He remembered his teacher showing the class a creepy film about a bug-eating plant that lured a fly or another insect to become its dinner. It first attracted the bug to its "flower" with a smell like sweet syrup or rotting meat. Inside, the fly or whatever would move down a narrowing, funnel-like passage with hairlike spikes that let the insect crawl in deeper but wouldn't allow it to go back. The bug would soon get trapped in the sticky "stomach" of the plant, where it would eventually become the plant's meal.

His imagination was getting the better of him. *It's a game, it's for fun, it's a twenty-five-buck bad joke,* he repeated to himself.

Calmer, he moved ahead.

In the next section, there were even shorter passages and even more doorways. He no longer had a clue whether he was making forward progress; but, since he hadn't circled back to the one-way gates, he assumed he was moving more or less ahead.

A new trio of one-way gates faced him. Through their sidewise bars, the halls beyond looked narrower still. But he no longer had a choice: it was either keep moving or start screaming until help came. He wasn't about to give in to a lousy trick. Past the center gate, the halls were barely wider than his shoulder span. Not liking the feeling of confinement, Little D kept his nervousness in check by moving steadily onward. The maze must end soon, he thought; soon he'd find the next exit.

But what he reached was yet another threefold gate. Not stopping to think, he pushed through the middle one. To his horror, he found the waiting passage was so tight that he could only move sideways. Desperately, he kept inching ahead.

He made one last forced turn and found himself up against a blank white wall—a dead end. He had run out of options. He was trapped. Little D managed to turn almost face-forward and run his hand over the wall, half expecting a doorknob or latch to reveal itself. But there was only smooth wall. Still, to his exploring hand, the wall felt *flimsy*.

Fury came to his rescue. *Messin' with my mind*, he thought. *They're playin' me, but I'm not buyin'*. He raised his fist and slammed it into the wall. His hand punched through so unexpectedly he tumbled past the balsa-wood and construction-paper barrier, sprawling on the floor with an impact that knocked the wind out of him.

After a minute, he stood up and looked around. He was perched on a ledge overlooking a three-floor drop-off. He remembered his climb up the seemingly endless flight of steps. The unlit space below was a pool of blackness. A thin tongue of metal extended across to a second ledge, below a now-familiar green-lit exit sign. The bridge was so narrow that a person could just stand on it with his two feet together. Crossing it would be little better than walking a tightrope at a circus. He realized this part of the path to successfully beating Chimera House was so openly dangerous that only a fool would risk life and limb trying to get across. This was clearly the point at which most visitors—those not already frightened off by snakes or worse—would bag it all and yell for help.

I've come too far to quit now, Little D decided. He knelt and put his palms on the metal surface, testing to see if it would shake or bounce. It seemed rock-solid.

Taking a deep breath to calm himself, the boy began to crawl along the foot-wide bridge. *Don't look down,* he warned himself. *Keep your eyes on the prize*—the exit sign. Hand over hand, shuffling on his knees, he inched along the catwalk. He resisted all temptation to glance down, keeping his eyes fixed on the promise of exit.

Once, in spite of his caution, his right knee almost slipped off the walk. He froze for a moment, feeling the least movement would tumble him off into the hungry darkness below. Vaguely he wondered how Chimera House got away with such dangerous setups. He could see why the owners kept it pretty much a secret.

When he stopped trembling from his near mishap, Little D crept forward. Assuring himself the worst was over, he made his careful way to the ledge—that was his goal. Only when he was sitting with his back to the stairwell door did he really begin breathing again. He felt like he had been holding his breath most of the way across.

The door to the last flight of stairs swung inward noiselessly. The sound of it locking behind him was no surprise.

He found himself at the bottom of a flight of steps of normal height that he quickly ascended. At the entrance to level five he hesitated. *What,* he wondered, *is the make-it-or-break-it secret that makes the end of this adventure too scary to complete?*

Only one way to find out.

Little D pushed open the final door.

Beyond was a huge space, dimly illuminated by lights recessed in the ceiling and scattered wall fixtures that glowed at the lowest power. The area had the vacant feel of an abandoned warehouse. Something about the emptiness made Little D more uneasy than he'd felt at any point so far.

He looked around for the expected exit sign, but couldn't locate it on the walls where the low-watt bulbs flickered a bit, as though the power on this floor was a sometime thing.

After a few hesitant steps forward, he stopped. A sound like a chuckle had emerged from the center of the space, where the lighting was at its worst and shadows seemed to thicken and curdle into curious shapes. Another laugh that sounded somehow faintly familiar to him reached his ears. Dead center of the vast room, the shadows shifted, re-forming themselves into a single new shape.

Frozen in place, the boy gaped. He could just make out the back of a massive, tall chair, as fancy as a throne. It looked like it was carved from ebony, and he saw a hint of blue velvet upholstery at the sides.

Someone was sitting in the chair. An arm appeared, and a hand motioned Little D forward. There were heavy gold rings on all four fingers and the thumb. When Little D remained where he was, the gesturing hand became more insistent.

Still he wouldn't budge.

With a sigh of disgust, the figure hauled itself out of the chair and turned to face Little D.

Toussaint's gold teeth flashed in the shadows; light gleamed on the strands of gold chain around his neck and danced off his rings.

"Hello, my young friend," Toussaint said, coming all the way around the chair to stand facing the boy, who was rigid with fear. The words were harmless. The man was smiling, but there was no warmth, no laughter, in the eyes that seemed to the boy as dark and dead as a shark's.

"What's the matter, boy?" Toussaint said. "Didn't expect to see me here? Didn't expect to see me ever, right?"

Little D was too frightened to move or make a sound.

"Cat got your tongue? Man, you look like you seen a

ghost." Then he chuckled without humor. "But that's the truth, *Little D*, little *friend, little Judas goat!*"

Little D managed a small shake of his head, denying the truth.

"Oh, I got me a witness," said the other, stepping closer to the boy. "The deceased. *Me!*"

"I nev—" was all that Little D got out before Toussaint held up his hand for silence.

"This house don't like liars," Toussaint said. "It's an old *honest* place. Makes you face what you've done straight up. That's why it's such a scary place. We all got secrets we don't want to own up to. But this place don't allow for none. People who built this place had power. I only found it through friends who have their own power. When you're dead, you don't have many ways to influence folks. But you can whisper things, put ideas in their heads, sometimes mess with their dreams. That's how I got Demond to decide he had to come here and he had to bring you. See, there ain't a lot of places where the dead can get their own back. But here I am and here you are and it's payback time."

Little D turned to run, but Toussaint's arms suddenly grew long and ropelike. They enfolded the boy in a smothering embrace.

Little D screamed, but the sound was drowned out by

Toussaint's roaring laugh, as all the lights went out. Held fast, the boy was tumbled into bottomless darkness.

On the first floor, Demond and the other three counted out their refunded money. The woman, now alone at the ticket desk, had handed the cash back to them with a smile.

"Just not scary enough?" she asked.

Antoine said, "Cardboard ghosts, skeletons on strings— nothin' much scary there."

"I sure didn't like those spiders and stuff," said Rachelle. "That was the worst."

"Except for nearly steppin' on some giant beetle, it was all pretty tame," said Lorelle.

"Well, not everyone comes away disappointed," said the woman, her smile deepening.

"Say, where's Little D?" Demond asked.

"He left before you came down," the woman said. "Said something on one of the top floors *really* scared him. He told me he didn't want to stay inside and he'd be out by the car." She riffled through some papers, signaling them it was time to be on their way. "Since you're our last guests of the day, we'll be closing up after you."

The others took the hint and left.

All but a handful of lights went out at the front of Chimera House.

Theirs was the only car in the lot. It sat in a pool of light, still locked up. There was no sign of Demond's brother.

They called his name but got no answer. The parking lot lights began to go out, row by row.

"Little D must still be in that place," his brother cried. He went back and began pounding on the firmly locked door of Chimera House.

The woman's voice answered from the little intercom by the door: "What is it?"

"My brother is still inside."

"He left. *I told you.* Security has motion sensors on every floor. There is no one here. Maybe he walked to the road and hitchhiked back. Boys do things like that. And they eventually turn up."

"But—"

"Good *night!*" There was a loud click. Then silence.

Muttering, Demond rejoined the others and explained what had happened.

They decided to go back to Detroit and see if, just maybe, Little D had fled home—though none of them could imagine anything frightening enough to scare him all the way back.

Eventually the police were involved, but no trace of

Little D was found initially. An investigation of Chimera House likewise failed to reveal any clue.

But the woman was right about one thing.

Little D did turn up.

His body was found in the alley where, days before, the body of Jean Marcelle Toussaint had been discovered.

To date, there are no suspects in either case.

Webs

It was the grossest thing Danny Parker had ever read. Of course, since the book was all about true and false gross-out factoids, he really wasn't surprised. His friend Marc had assured Danny that everyone swallowed about eight spiders a year while they were asleep—and accidentally ate many more in foods like rice, vegetables, pepper, and so on. Marc was forever teasing Danny about his hatred of spiders, but his stupid tickles or plastic spiders didn't bother Danny that much. The idea that he might routinely be swallowing spiders at night really made his skin crawl. What the book reported wasn't good news; in some ways, it was worse than Marc said. He wished his friend had kept his mouth shut about the need for keeping your mouth shut at night.

Webs

What super grossed him out was that the book indicated Marc was right, in a way. You *could* eat what amounted to eight spiders a year. They wouldn't be live spiders—just parts of spiders mixed in with other stuff. But whole or pieces, alive or dead, the thought of consuming that many spiders a year totally turned Danny's stomach.

Unbelievably, the book said that there were even people who deliberately ate spiders. In Thailand, people ate big, hairy, poisonous tarantulas. They roasted them and served them in coconut cream with lime leaves.

Yuck! Danny thought. *Too much information.*

He closed the book, not sure if reading in the moving car or the winding mountain road was giving him the start of a headache. At least Marissa, his little sister, continued sleeping. She'd been alternately fussing and singing a song that she had learned in day care (and quickly discovered annoyed her big brother):

> *There was an old woman*
> *Who swallowed a spider*
> *That wriggled and jiggled*
> *And tickled inside her. . . .*

For the time being, with her singsong voice still and the

book shut, Danny turned his mind away from spiders. He focused on the scenery instead.

To the right of the car was an unbroken green wall of piney wood; on the left was a sharp drop-off to the water far below. If Danny craned his neck, he could see sunlight flash off its ripples. The road had been following the stream for nearly half an hour. But after ten more minutes, his father turned off to the right on a side road and they left the creek behind.

Another ten minutes, and his dad slowed, then parked the car on a patch of gravel in front of the big, gray house that was their summer rental. Even before he climbed out of the car, Danny sensed something creepy about the place, though he couldn't say why, exactly. It was old: The gray paint and white trim were peeling in strips. The roof and porch and steps had a thick covering of pine needles and dried leaves from the woods that were primarily pines and oaks. The trees grew all around and actually seemed to shoulder right up to the back of the building, so it was half in sunlight, half in shadow. The place gave the impression that it hadn't been lived in, or even looked after, for years. *Perfect place for a haunting,* the boy thought sourly, surprised at how deep his instant dislike was running.

It was early afternoon on a warm July day. The trip from Raleigh, North Carolina, had been pleasant (when not intruded on by spider songs or factoids). Marissa had remained asleep in her car seat as things were unpacked. Danny guessed she had worn herself out crying through the night in the too-warm hotel room near the airport— flight delays had trapped them overnight. At last they were at the house that would be theirs for the next two months while Professor Andrew Parker, his dad, finished his book on economics and Carolyn, Danny's mother, painted landscapes that would eventually be displayed in several galleries where her work was well known.

Danny wasn't too sure about this adventure, but at the age of nine, he was in no position to argue his parents out of a summer away from his friends, the community pool, barbecues, and baseball in the park. And it was no use pointing out to them some of the disturbing things he'd learned about the place. They were in New Hebron Valley, which had twice been the scene of unusual spider infestations in years past. He'd Googled the place out of curiosity and learned more than he wanted to know. Several of the Web sites he visited spoke of an extinct Indian tribe—the name apparently forgotten—which had "worshipped a goddess not unlike Spider Woman or Spider Grandmother, figures well known in the American Southwest."

When white men had first come to the area, the boy discovered, they had quickly wiped out the natives with bullets and smallpox. The last medicine woman of the lost people, it was said, had put a curse on the valley, promising that spiders would continue to make life a misery for anyone who settled there.

Comparing the Internet accounts, Danny decided that, while many of the background stories were doubtful, the spiders were the real thing. He read enough archived news reports to know that infestations of spiders, as well as occasional deaths due to the bites of toxic species, were all higher here than in any other part of the state. And, according to his online resources, they were going to be vacationing in the worst part of the valley.

The one time he did mention it to his father, Professor Parker had simply murmured, "That's interesting," and the discussion had died.

Trying another tactic, he asked his mother, "What am I supposed to *do* all summer?"

"You'll find plenty to do, trust me," Carolyn assured him.

Now this first sight of the house was anything but reassuring for no reason he could put a finger on. The generous porch ran all the way across the front of the house and extended down both sides. Above, a narrow balcony with a waist-high railing circled the second story. Two doors, one on either end of the building, gave access to the balcony.

But there was something about the place that gave Danny the uncanny feeling that he was being watched by several sets of eyes. Yet the windows were empty of anything except half-drawn shades or the hint of yellowing lace curtains; nothing stirred but a few wind-riffled leaves on the porch steps.

"The Mertons told me they'd leave a key under the flowerpot to the right of the door," Danny's father said. The boy had overheard him talking a month earlier with the couple who owned the house. They had left nearly a week ago for a summer-long vacation in Europe but didn't want the house to stand empty. Making it a summer rental had worked out fine for both parties. The Parkers had never actually met the owners; all business had been done over the phone and computer. The first real meeting would take place after the Mertons returned to reclaim their home at summer's end.

With a grunt, Andrew Parker tilted back the heavy pot filled with dusty, faded geraniums and spoke to Danny, who had followed him onto the porch. "Grab the key, will you?"

Danny handed over the key as soon as Andrew set the pot back in place. Walking a little way down the porch, Danny peered through a window into a living room filled with odd pieces of furniture that didn't match very well.

Everything suggested no one had lived in the place for years. But Danny knew, from something his parents said, that the Mertons were pretty old. And he understood, from visiting his grandmother's house, that old people sometimes let stuff slide—often because they didn't see too clearly how messy a place was getting.

For just a minute, Danny thought he saw something dark move near a picture on the far wall. But it was hard to see through the streaked, grimy glass. The air underneath the porch roof was hot and dusty. There was a stillness and a staleness that made Danny feel as though the house was caught in some kind of invisible box, like one of the glass cages in the reptile room at the zoo where they put snakes and the oversized spiders that *totally* creeped him out.

Once they'd unpacked the car and he'd put his junk in the upstairs room he'd chosen as his bedroom, he was startled by a shriek and then a prolonged wail from Marissa, who had gone down the hall to look at her new room. By the time he got to her bedroom, his sister was being comforted by their mother while their father looked at the girl's wrist. "That's a pretty big welt," Andrew said. "I'd better get some antiseptic." This started Marissa crying again.

"What happened?" Danny asked.

"She says she was bitten by a spider," his mother said. Mom was seated on the bed, hugging Marissa, who was making sounds somewhere between sniffles and hiccups. While their father doctored the wound, their mother tried to get Marissa to give her details of what had happened. But all the girl could say was that it was big, it had jumped at her from a corner of the closet, bit her, and scurried away when she screamed and shook her arm. Andrew Parker got a flashlight and checked the closet and everywhere a spider might be hiding, but he found nothing. Even watching from across the room, Danny could see that there was a puffy pink swelling about the size of a quarter on his sister's wrist. "Spider bites can be dangerous, Carolyn. I think we need to go into town and have someone look at it."

Danny felt like saying "I warned you," but he knew now wasn't the time.

His parents wanted him to come along, but Danny said he wasn't feeling well and just wanted to lie down. That was partly true: Traces of his headache and stomach upset had lingered. Mostly, he wasn't eager to get back in the car. Anxious to get Marissa's wound checked out, his parents agreed, though they made him promise to stay put and not go exploring or take any chances.

When they were gone, Danny began wandering through the house. Feeling thoroughly bored, he recalled that his father said the old couple kept rabbits as pets. Signing the rental agreement, the Parkers had agreed to be responsible for taking care of them while the Mertons were away. Well, this at least sounded interesting. Danny went to look for the rabbits. At the back of the house, he found a large wire-mesh cage on wooden legs that he guessed was the rabbit hutch. But it was swathed in spider silk.

He snapped off a bit of pine branch from an overhanging tree and began swiping it back and forth across the wire sides of the hutch, brushing away the veiling webs, alert for spiders. Thankfully, he didn't see any.

There were no rabbits. Although the water dish was empty, the food dish was filled with dry pellets. Then Danny saw two web-encased bundles in the back corner of the enclosure. Each was about the size of a silk-wrapped doll. The webbing had woven them together into something like Siamese twin cocoons. He unlatched and lifted the lid of the hutch. On impulse, still holding the pine branch, he turned it around and poked at one bundle with the stick end. The jagged point slipped through the webbing, then hit something solid. Feeling both *should* and *shouldn't* impulses, he let his curiosity win—though he was half afraid that it might be a spider's egg sac that would suddenly release a flood of tiny, crawly horrors. (Boy, was he regretting that nature show he'd watched a month before!) He snagged a clot of the web and pulled back, ready to drop the stick and hightail it to the house if he unleashed a torrent of baby spiders.

But all that was revealed, when he'd pulled the bit of web free, was a patch of dusty-gray, very stiff fur. Distressed, but determined to follow through, he continued to unwrap the bundle with the stick. What was there was pretty much what he'd expected: the mummified remains of a rabbit. The small carcass was thin—it seemed mostly fur and bones—and regarded him with an eye that had dried up and was really just an indent. It looked like it had been drained dry, like the papery remains of flies and moths he'd sometimes find stuck in a web in some corner of the garage at home. As far as he was concerned, one of the worst things about spiders was how they ate, suffocating their victims in silk and sucking the juice out of them.

The thought made him nervous. He pulled back and let the lid drop into place with a crash. *Poor things,* he thought. They'd fallen victim to what must be some *really big* spiders, whose handiwork—their webs—was everywhere, even though none of them was willing to show itself.

The breeze strengthened. It set the pine needles overhead and around him rustling. It wasn't much of a stretch—especially after discovering the hutch and its contents—to imagine the trees swarming with spiders, each of them rubbing pairs of legs together, anticipating something far more generous and juicy than two rabbit carcasses. His always overactive imagination envisioned hundreds—thousands—of eight-legged horrors positioning themselves to drop like a living, squirming net on his head.

Having totally freaked himself out, he retreated from the backyard and the shivering trees. Since he still wasn't ready to go back inside the house, he went around to the front. To his disgust, he now realized there were webs everywhere between the porch railings and clustered wherever support posts met roof. *Time for Bugbusters spray.* He hoped his mom had packed plenty.

But he wasn't prepared to go spider hunting this afternoon. He'd had enough of spiders. Since there was no sign of his parents, he hoped Marissa was all right. She could be a royal pest, but she was only a little kid—and the spider bite looked nasty. *What a heckuva start to this vacation.* But then, all the spider alerts had been pretty much a turnoff to him from the get-go.

Forgetting his parents' warning, he decided to follow the twisty access back to the main road. If he was lucky, he might find a way down to the stream below. It was the sort of adventure his parents wouldn't approve of—but, for the moment, he was free of their input.

He ambled along the road, enjoying the light and warmth, and feeling, for the first time since they'd arrived, that he really was on vacation. When he reached the bend in the road where the stream reappeared, he paused, picked up a handful of small stones, and began tossing them into the water. The road was so high above the creek bed, he could barely hear the *pleuf, pleuf, pleuf* of the stones hitting the water and sinking.

He looked around but couldn't find a path down the slope that looked even faintly safe.

He continued along the road.

Crickets sang, birds twittered, things—lizards probably—whisked through the underbrush. He could hear clearly now the gurgle of the stream below. The road curved back and forth on itself in easy bends at first. Then he came to the series of hairpin turns that had worried his dad earlier. Below the road edge, the slope was a ferocious drop-off, almost a sheer plunge to the water below. The creek bed was narrower; the water flowed more rapidly, raising impressive ripples and lots of foam. The water looked deeper and darker than it had higher up.

It was at the third switchback that he discovered a disturbance in the shrubbery. Some broken branches and scattered dirt and stones suggested something—probably a car—had plowed through the underbrush. But most of the greenery was of the rubbery and resilient kind that would spring back into place after a vehicle had rolled over it. Little growth seemed to have been permanently damaged by whatever had passed through. If a person hadn't been as close as Danny was, or wasn't actually looking for signs of a mishap, they'd be easy to miss.

Stepping carefully off the asphalt, the boy pushed apart springy boughs, following a faint trail that grew more obvious when he got farther from the road edge. Where the growth seemed older and sturdier, he found several spots where thicker branches had been snapped off bushes and lay dead and brown. The trunk of one hardy pine showed a gash where it had clearly been sideswiped by a car or whatever it was that had left flecks of blue paint embedded in the bark.

Danny was so busy searching for clues that he almost walked off the edge of the gorge, which dropped some hundred feet to the stream below. The water, trapped between facing cliffs, looked to be its swiftest and deepest here.

Peering down, one arm hooked around a sturdy young tree, Danny studied the space below him. It looked like a narrow footpath ran alongside the churning water, though he could spot no way to get down.

The longer he looked, the surer he was that there was something just below the rippling, foaming water. He was certain he could make out a swatch of blue and a crimson oval. Was it the red plastic taillight of a blue car? He wondered. Had he been checking out the site of an accident, where a car had missed the turn, whipped through the undergrowth, and then plunged into the rapids? What he'd found so far made that easy to believe.

He had to get down for a closer look, he decided.

He returned to the road, noting with satisfaction that, beyond the dangerous curve, his way was now a steep descent. He wished he'd paid closer attention on the drive up, but he had been impatient to see where most of their summer would be spent—and had been tired of sitting quietly, trying to keep from waking up his sister. Now he vaguely wondered how she and their parents were faring. They'd been gone an awfully long time. Still, it looked like he might just have a chance to check out what he believed was the scene of some accident.

What if there's a body in the car? he wondered. The idea excited and repelled him at the same time. When he thought about it the notion seemed unlikely. People would have noticed if someone was missing—someone local—because who else would be using a private road? Of course, he had heard on the news about cars and people that had not been found for weeks or months, even, after they were reported missing. And those kinds of stories usually involved some kind of wilderness area—like the place he was in now.

Well, it didn't matter until he got a better look.

The road continued to dip. He kept an ear out for the return of the family van, but the day was silent except for the *buzz-hum-chirp* of the natural world. At the bottom of the hill, he found a dirt trail leading into the woods in the direction of the stream. A short way into the thicket, he began to hear the rushing waters.

When he pushed past a couple of trees, he found himself in luck: The path from the road ran into a trail that veered to his right and left, following the edge of the creek. Without pausing, he started off on the right-hand branch—the one that would take him back to the spot he wanted to check out.

He went slowly. The path was wet and slippery from mist thrown off by the rapids. But soon enough he was almost to the point where the stream flowed fastest and deepest. The trail seemed even slicker and narrower here. He edged along it with his back to the damp rock wall, his arms spread-eagled.

From far above, he thought he heard shifting gears as a car made its way up the hill. He guessed his parents were returning. They'd probably be freaked out to find him gone, but there was no way he could hurry. And he was so close—he *had* to find out what was in the water. He just hoped they wouldn't get too mad. He'd tell them he got lost in the woods. They couldn't blame him (too much) for that, he reasoned. *Of course*, he remembered, *they told me not to go wandering off. Yeah, there will probably be trouble. Oh, well. Too late now to turn back.*

The path widened a tad above the churning water in the pool, where the stream gushed into the roughly circular basin, swirled around, then raced out a narrow spout of rock to continue its journey downhill. Dropping to his hands and knees, he peered over the trail edge into the water below.

During the time it had taken him to climb down and reach the spot, the level of water had dropped a bit. Now he could make out just above the surface of the restless water what was clearly the hatchback of a blue station wagon. The license was North Carolina in design. Two red oval taillights were visible, one a bit higher than the other, as if the car had come to rest tilted at an angle. Unless the driver had jumped for it as the car crashed through the growth above, Danny doubted anyone could have survived the plunge. He had a hunch the car was solidly wedged between the rocky walls of the stream. Even if someone *had* made it into the water alive, the side doors of the car were probably jammed shut, and there was no sign that the back hatch had been released.

He lay flat on the wet stone to get an even closer look. Oddly enough, the back window seemed to have curtains— gray, lacy ones. Leaning dangerously far down, he could

just make out that they weren't curtains at all—they were spiderwebs.

He pulled back from the rim and stood up as quickly as he dared. Then he began his retreat along the path. When he reached the road, he ran as fast as the mostly uphill way would allow.

The family van was parked on the gravel turnaround in front of the house.

"Mom, Dad," he called into the silence of the living room. A moment later, his father charged down the stairs.

"Where have you been?" he demanded. "I was just about to call the police. Isn't it enough that we've got Marissa to worry about, without you adding to it?"

Andrew's anger was beyond anything Danny had expected. "I went for a short hike, and I got lost."

His father's face softened a bit. His voice just sounded tired now. "You shouldn't go off wandering. Your mother has been frantic."

"Um, how's Marissa?" the boy asked.

"Mom's with her now. The doctor put her on antibiotics, but she's running a fever. She sleeps most of the time, but when she wakes up, she's really out of it. The doctor said if there isn't a change soon, he'll hospitalize her." Now Danny could hear real worry in his voice.

"Dad, there's a car in the water—" the boy began. But his dad didn't hear, having already started upstairs to check on his wife and daughter.

Uncertain what to do, but thinking it best to stay out of his parents' hair, Danny wandered into the kitchen. He was starving after the day's adventure, and there was no one to warn him about spoiling his dinner. He slathered two pieces of bread with mayonnaise and, feeling devil-may-care, fixed himself a bologna, olive loaf, and Swiss cheese sandwich, with double portions of all the fillings. Taking the sandwich and a big glass of milk out onto the back porch, he sat in one of the old wooden rockers.

As he ate, the shadows crept from underneath the pines around the house, and he found himself listening for the sounds of scuttling legs or the tickle of a small, furry touch on the back of his neck. His eyes strayed upward. The sheltered roof space overhead was thick with cobwebs. He couldn't be sure in the fading light, but he thought he saw dark shapes moving behind the screen of webbing.

He gobbled the rest of his sandwich, washed it down with the last of the milk, and went inside, vowing that he'd return tomorrow, armed with a ladder, a broom, and a full can of insecticide, and make the porch a spider-free zone.

Dinner wasn't much—just a thrown-together salad, some soup, and a plate of cold cuts. Danny wasn't hungry, and his parents, worried about Marissa, didn't notice his lack of appetite. They gave him a halfhearted warning about not wandering off and remembering that the woods held often unexpected dangers.

He mumbled agreement—they were clearly too pre-occupied with Marissa's condition to get worked up over his earlier disobedience.

His mother hastily cleared the table and then said, "I'm going up to check on her." His dad remained, sipping his coffee, staring out the window at the moonlit pines.

It seemed a good time to tell of his discovery, so Danny began to talk about the accident scene he was sure he'd found. At first his father didn't seem to be tuning in, but the more details Danny provided, the more interested he became. He didn't seem to notice that Danny's tale of detective work was quite different from his earlier story of getting lost on a hike.

"What color did you say the back part of the car was?"

"Real dark blue—like Uncle John's car."

His father suddenly got up and went to the desk in the corner of the living room. A minute later he pulled out a file folder. He brought it back to the kitchen table. He rummaged through it, and finally drew out a color photo. "Blue like this?" he asked, sliding the photo across to Danny.

It was a picture of their summer house. Danny remembered being shown it when his parents were first arranging to rent the space. The photo had a picture of the Mertons—a sixtyish couple—in the driveway, smiling and waving. Between them and the house, the boy could clearly see the side and back of a deep blue station wagon with oval taillights.

"Do you think—" Danny began.

"I don't know what to think. I'd hate to find out this is the reason the Mertons never checked in with us when we arrived."

His father took the photo back, studied it a moment longer, and then got his cell phone from the desk. Danny heard him asking information for the number of the local sheriff's office. He couldn't hear more, because his father walked out onto the front porch and closed the door behind him.

When he returned a few minutes later, he simply said, "The sheriff is sending out a deputy to check first thing in the morning. He says it would be hopeless to investigate in the dark. And, if it is the Mertons' car, it's too late for a few hours to make a difference. He'll come to the house first, for you, so you can show him the exact spot where you spotted the car. Now I'm going up to look in on the girls."

Danny stared again at the photo. It saddened him to think that, if there was a body—no, *bodies*—in the car, it wouldn't be some nameless, faceless accident victims, but might well be the two friendly looking people in the photo.

The deputy was at their door at eight-thirty. Danny, eager to help and excited to be a part of a police investigation, had been dressed and ready to go for an hour. His parents hardly seemed to register the deputy's arrival: Marissa had had a restless night, and they were debating taking her back to the doctor.

Danny's father spoke briefly to the officer and gave him the photo they'd looked at the night before.

Danny showed the officer where he thought the car had torn through the underbrush before going over the edge. The man jotted some notes, then had Danny lead him to the path along the river. To the boy's disappointment, the man ordered him to stay put while he investigated what he, too, now seemed convinced was a crash site.

When he returned twenty minutes later, Danny saw that he seemed shaky. The boy suspected the last bit of water-slicked trail had gotten to the deputy, the way it had scared Danny the day before. But he said nothing.

On their way back to the patrol car, the deputy said, "Gonna be a bear fishing out that car—probably need a crane."

Danny wanted to watch the retrieval the next day, but

his parents refused. Marissa was not much better; he had to go with them to the doctor's office, where he realized he'd left his Sony PSP at the house, so he had to poke through old copies of *Today's Health* and *Wellness for Kids* or just pace up and down impatiently.

There were still police cars, an ambulance, and a monstrous crane that blocked the road for a while when the family returned home. Around dinnertime, the deputy drove up and asked to speak to Danny's dad "in private."

They went out on the front porch. Marissa was asleep upstairs, and his mother was fixing dinner, so no one had noticed when Danny stood beside a partly open window to hear what the deputy had to report.

"It was Sam and Ida Merton," the man said. "They must've missed the turn, sailed off the cliff. Never had a chance. Car was pinned between two rocks like it was caught in a vise. Nearly broke the cable before we hauled it up. Odd, since Sam had driven that road since Hector was a pup."

"Maybe he had a heart attack," Danny's father suggested.

"Could be. Everything will be checked out. Looks pretty much like an accident, clear and simple. Only funny thing: The inside of the car was filled with spiderwebs."

"Spiderwebs?"

"Yeah—covering all the windows. Bodies wrapped in

them, too. And there were plenty of spiders—bigger than any I recall ever seeing—in the car. Drowned, of course. The car was filled with water. Someone suggested that it might have held some air pockets long enough for the spiders to get in a little last weaving. But what so many were doing in the car is a puzzle. I suppose it's possible they contributed to the accident, though that's pretty unlikely. Well, it's up to the medical examiner now."

The two men exchanged a few more words, then the deputy left. Danny was innocently playing his PSP at the dining room table when his dad came back inside.

He asked about what the deputy had said, but his father didn't want to talk, giving him only vague answers, and then went for a quick check on Marissa before their meal.

The next morning, Danny set to work freeing the back porch of spiders, which he linked to the deaths of their land-lords. From the kitchen he could hear his parents' debate over continuing to stay, given the Mertons' accident and the slow response of Marissa's illness to the doctor's prescriptions, though she was improving.

Standing on the stepladder, Danny liberally sprayed the canopy of webs with insecticide, waited a few minutes, then, moving the ladder to one side, raked the webs with the broom. He was grimly satisfied to see shriveled-up spiders fall like rain onto the floorboards. Most were small, but some were distressingly large. Some of the bigger ones were still twitching and seemed to glare at him with their multifaceted eyes. These he quickly slammed out of existence with his trusty broom. When the webs were down and the spiders dead, he swept all the remains off the porch.

His mother stepped out onto the porch. "Thanks for helping, hon," she said, clearly meaning only sweeping up. "Your dad is on the phone with a nephew of the Mertons'. We've decided to go home tomorrow. This trip has turned into a nightmare." She gave him a thin smile. "Great summer, huh? *Summer bummer* is more like it. We know you'll be disappointed, but we'll make it up, I promise."

Danny shrugged. Finding the car had seemed exciting. But finding out it was the Mertons inside had been awful. And he wasn't going to be sorry to leave this spider-infested house behind.

"We'll leave early tomorrow," she said. "Marissa should be well enough to travel by then."

"I'll be ready."

He was, in fact, pretty well packed before he went to bed. He felt relieved to know they'd be leaving this freakish place behind.

But his good feeling didn't bring a good night's sleep. Danny tossed and turned as his dreams grew more and more confusing and disturbing. Sam and Ida Merton rose out of a silky, shiny river in front of him, where he sat on the edge of the stream, dangling his feet. They hovered in the air, their movements herky-jerky, until he saw they were really puppets dangling from the arms of multilegged, shadowy puppeteers. Then he was in the dining room of the Merton house, where his father was trying to talk into a cell phone but kept complaining that he couldn't hear— when suddenly the phone split apart and a torrent of spiders poured out, covering his father and the tabletop. Then his mother was warning him not to go into the woods, where the trees were clotted with spiderwebs and alive with the rustling of a million furry bodies. These suddenly began dropping in a black rain on him as he ran along a path that grew narrower and narrower. Then he was in the backseat of a sinking station wagon. In the front seat, Marissa, her back to him, was singing

> *There was an old woman*
> *Who swallowed a spider*
> *That wriggled and jiggled*
> *And tickled inside her.*

Water began gushing into the car. It was thick and gray with floating web strands, and they were swarming with tiny spiders. The car was flooding; he could no longer hear or see Marissa. He was awash in a sea of spiders. He opened his mouth to scream and swallowed a mouthful of chill water thick with spiders and webbing.

Danny woke up gagging and choking and coughing. Like he had swallowed something. But then he decided it was only a part of his dream—and a dry throat—at work. The digital clock showed 3:14 A.M. Only a few hours until they'd load themselves in the van and head home.

His throat still felt scratchy and coughy. He decided to go down and get some ice water from the fridge. When he stepped out into the hall, it seemed darker than he remembered. He glanced at the ceiling light. It was swathed in spiderwebs, the gray veiling so thick that it cast the upstairs hallway into semishadow. Now, as he looked around, Danny saw that spiderwebs festooned everything—pictures on the wall, light fixtures, the odd table or shelf lining the hall. The webs were *all over.* He touched his fingers to a wall, and they came away web-sticky. His bare feet, he found to his horror, were picking up clots of spiderwebs that covered the floor, like a second carpet.

How did all this happen so fast? Danny wondered. It grossed him out. When he stopped and listened, he could hear the *scuttle-flutter* of countless spider legs overhead, underfoot, all around. But he couldn't see the creatures—just their webs.

Marissa's door was ajar. Suddenly fearful for his sister, he nudged open her door.

"Marissa," he asked in a whisper, "you okay?"

He moved closer to the bed. His sister was a shadowy bundle on the bed. She didn't seem to be moving. *Has the infection from the spider bite gotten worse?* he wondered. *Should I wake Mom and Dad?* He reached down to where the top of her head was just visible above the covers, to feel for fever—the way his parents did. Then he yanked his hand back as though he'd touched a live wire. Her skin felt dry and rough and sticky. In pulling back his hand, he caused the blanket to slip free, exposing what should have been—but wasn't—her face. Her head was a featureless gray blank, like a discolored egg. Shaking, he peered closer and realized the figure of his sister was completely wrapped in spiderwebs. He started pulling away the clingy strands, but he stopped when he realized that his effort was useless. His sister's face, under the web, belonged to a papery, hollow-eyed mummy, from which the life had long since been drained away.

Screeching at the top of his lungs, he burst into his parents' room, but stopped on the threshold. The bed, walls, floor, and ceiling were a churning darkness. The sliding glass doors, unshaded, were blanketed with a living curtain that the bright moonlight revealed as countless swarming eight-legged bodies of every size in restless silhouette.

He felt a tickle, then another, then a dozen on his neck and arms. The first spiders were already claiming him as the dark mass advanced on him like an ebony sea at flood tide.

Frantically brushing the advance scouts from him, he fled.

Numerous webs had been strung across the stairway, but he pushed through the flimsy barriers, flicking off the weavers that sometimes clung to the bits of webbing that stuck to his face and chest and legs.

The ground floor was a nightmare of webs. He windmilled his arms, always moving, struggling to where he thought the front door was hidden.

A rustling, like a powerful wind through the treetops back home, alerted him. Glancing up, he saw swarms of spiders that had followed him downstairs seething across the overhead network of webs, clearly intent on cutting him off from escape. He ripped through layer after layer of the gray matting in front of him. And pulled apart the last strands. He grasped the front doorknob, ignoring the repulsive stickiness that coated it.

Then he had the door open and was half running, half stumbling across the web-shrouded porch and down the steps onto the blessedly open road. He could think of nothing more than running. He dimly registered the family van, its windows and wheel wells web-choked. He thought of the Mertons running for their lives in the car that the spiders had already claimed as their territory.

He ran until he reached the main road and was nearly run down by a pickup whose driver stopped, collected the hysterical boy from the side of the road, and rushed him to the hospital. Which was where the deputy and sheriff came to start sorting out the story. As he drifted in and out of sleep in a hospital bed, he was aware of two things:

The deputy repeating over and over, "Ain't never seen nothing like that."

And the tickle in his throat that kept bringing him half awake, coughing, until the irritation moved deeper into him, and the worst of his coughing stopped, and he slept. He woke up once, and came partly alert long enough to realize the sensation had moved down into his stomach, where it wriggled and jiggled and tickled inside him.

Dollhouse

It was Katie who found the dollhouse in the basement of the family's new home. She had been told to play outside while her parents and sister and brother unpacked cartons of clothes, dishes, kitchenware, and so on. But Katie was often not one to do as she was told. The basement—big and poorly lit and crammed with potentially dangerous things like rusty saws and a rake with a broken and splintered handle and such—was not a place she should be poking around in, her parents insisted. Their saying no just made going to explore that much more exciting.

So she waited until her parents and her older siblings, Carla and Stuart, were all busy outside or at the other end of the house. Then she slipped through the basement door in the hallway and, closing it quietly behind her, hurried down the steep steps to the big space, where only a soft gray light seeped through high windows filmed with dust and cobwebs. At the bottom of the stairs was a light switch. She flicked it, and three dirty, fly-specked bare bulbs overhead flared into life, revealing the full extent of the jumble. Her parents had bought the house as a "fixer-upper." They had done a lot of cleaning, repairing, and painting in the rooms on the first and second floors, where the family would live. But there was considerable work ahead just sorting out the basement junk and cleaning up what would, she knew, eventually become her dad's workshop.

Rummaging through the stacks of stuff all around, she discovered the expected broken furniture, rusted gardening tools, and boxes of everything from moldy books to yellowing Christmas cards with dates twenty years old or more.

She investigated further, sometimes pushing objects or cartons aside—careful not to upset anything that would make noise and alert her parents to what she was doing.

One corner was walled off by stacks of boxes filled with old papers in file folders. But, between two tall stacks, she glimpsed something big and draped with a white sheet. Curious, she began tugging and pushing at the file boxes, until she had pried open a passage just wide enough to squeeze through. All at once, a carton tumbled over with a loud noise. She held her breath and waited, sure that someone would come downstairs to investigate, but no one upstairs seemed to have heard. After a few moments, she continued shouldering her way past the boxes. Then she was through; she was in a squarish open space with a crude table at its center. It was merely a thick sheet of plywood mounted on two wooden sawhorses. On top was a large shape completely covered with a sheet. For minutes she tried to guess what lay hidden under the dips and rises of the shroud. Then, impatient, she gave a tug and the cloth slid to the cement floor with a whispery sound.

The dollhouse was amazing. Katie couldn't give a name to the style of it—she just knew it was old-fashioned. In a way, it reminded her of the house where Mary Poppins came to work her magic in the movie—or like that big old house where the Addams Family acted out their weirdness in Nick at Nite reruns of the old television series. There were double windows on each side of the front door (which had a tiny black wreath on it) and twin windows on the second floor, with a single window above the front door.

Katie could just barely move around behind the platform the dollhouse perched on. And she really had to squeeze along the narrow alley where the plywood was pushed pretty close to the basement wall. But it was worth the effort: There was no back wall on the dollhouse, so the inside was fully revealed.

There were four main rooms—two above, two below—divided by a stairway that rose from the downstairs hall to the upstairs hall.

The two downstairs rooms seemed to be a dining room and a kind of living room or den. The dining room was covered with brown patterned wallpaper, and the ceiling was a pale near white. The floor was polished bare wood. The furniture included a dining table with four chairs, a china cabinet against one wall, and a long buffet against the other. Curtains of some soft, shiny brown material framed the windows. The table was clearly set for three.

Across the narrow hallway, the den was covered with a sea-green carpet, while the walls were papered in dark green. A couch and chairs were pulled up close to a fireplace. There were bookcases on one wall and a wooden desk, holding an antique typewriter, with an office-style chair next to the desk. Near the fireplace was a clunky old radio. Without TV and a Blu-ray player and a game console, Katie thought, evenings in a real house like that would be pretty dull.

The most interesting thing here was the tiny figure of a man, reading a book, smoking a pipe, seated in a soft green armchair. A face with a thin mustache and tiny round glasses gazed at the open book. A floor lamp stood beside the chair. He was wearing a jacket of a pale material that showed up the black armband on his left upper sleeve.

Upstairs were two bedrooms. The main one was pale gray. A silvery carpet covered the floor, while white curtains hung at the windows. The room contained a dressing table, a bureau, and a double bed with a cream-colored comforter.

On the upstairs landing was the figure of a woman whose pretty face was set off by long red hair fixed in a style from long ago. She wore old-fashioned clothes—skirt, blouse, and shoes—that were all black.

Has someone died? Katie wondered. In old movies, when people dressed in black and wore black armbands—there was the wreath on the front door, too—it meant someone had died. The woman was facing the closed door of the second bedroom.

It's a girl's room, Katie decided. A pink spread covered the bed, while just above was the framed image, barely larger than a postage stamp, of a painting she'd seen in a Los Angeles museum on vacation the past summer. The painting, titled *Pinkie*, showed a young girl, standing on a hill long ago, her silky skirts blown by the wind. She had a flat, wide hat; its ribbons were untied and rippling in the breeze. Katie remembered her mother reading a guidebook that explained the girl was nicknamed Pinkie. She was eleven when the painting had been completed; she died a few months later. *Weird*, thought Katie, *all that black, and the picture of someone who had died when she was just a little girl.*

Letting her eyes take in other details of the room, she saw tiny books and games arranged neatly on a low bookcase. A tall wardrobe cabinet was placed beside a small dressing table with ruffles around the skirting. This held a tiny mirror and pink plastic comb.

Curious, Katie checked each room again but could find no little girl figure. *Has it gotten lost?* she wondered. Then an odd thought occurred to her: *Could the absent child be the one who died? Is she the reason for the man's black armband, the lady's black outfit, and the black wreath on the front door?* Then she told herself, *That's silly. Dolls don't die!*

But she recalled a story her grandmother, who had come from England, told about a doll's ghost. When a little girl's best-loved china doll was broken beyond repair, the tiny ghost of the doll lingered, seen only by the girl. When there was a fire in the house, the doll woke the child, and she was able to save her family. After that, the doll's ghost went away forever.

Nana swore that it was true. Just to test things, Katie broke her third-favorite doll to bits. No ghost showed up. She decided her nana was just telling fairy tales.

"Katie!" Her mother's voice, faint but clear, came from somewhere overhead. Startled, Katie began edging out from behind the dollhouse. When she reached the corner of the table, she heard her mother's voice—fainter now, suggesting she was looking for Katie outside the house—probably in the front yard. It wouldn't be long before someone thought to look in the basement. Hastily she gathered up the dust sheet and flung it over the house. She wasn't sure why, but she wanted to keep the dollhouse her secret for as long as she could.

When the little house was shrouded, she wormed her way back through the piled file boxes. She put out the basement lights and then hurried upstairs, stumbling once or twice because it had grown quite late and the fading light through the grimy windows, as well as the few dusty overhead bulbs, left the stairs dangerously dark. The clutter below was only a mass of looming or pooling shadows.

At the head of the stairs, Katie listened carefully to be sure no one was in the hallway outside. Then she risked opening the door a bit, peering through the crack. Deciding that the coast was clear, she stepped out and closed the door softly behind her.

She hurried down the hall to the kitchen. Her father was just straightening up, palms pressed into the small of his back, relieved to be done with whatever he had taken care of under the sink.

"Hi, Daddy," she said. He spun around. "Hey, princess. Mom's looking everywhere for you. Where have you been?"

She shrugged.

"Well, Mom's in the front yard. Go tell her you're back from Wonderland or wherever. I think we'll call it a day and go for pizza. Sound good?"

"Sounds great," she called over her shoulder as she went to find her mother.

The pizza at Lonnie's was cheesy, deep dish, with extra cheese buried in the thick crusts—Katie's favorite. But she couldn't get the dollhouse off her mind. She was eager to explore it further and perhaps tease out some of its secrets.

The next day, while her mother and the older kids were shopping and her father was repairing the brick barbecue pit at the back of the yard, Katie slipped into the basement. Eagerly, she uncovered the dollhouse. Trying for a better view, she climbed onto one of the two plywood planks that supported the house, being careful to test that it would hold her. The thick wood felt as secure as solid ground. She particularly wanted to have a closer look at the figures and furniture. But when she reached for the mother doll in the upstairs hall, her fingers ran into something that felt almost like a sheet of plastic protecting the open side of the house. There was no real covering; it was just a sensation that the air had grown almost solid. When she gave a gentle push, the barrier yielded a little, but she had to push really hard to reach past it. With the feeling of something tearing, her hand suddenly punched all the way through, though she felt as if the unseen wall was closed up around her wrist, like the air was healing itself. *Weird*, she thought.

She pulled the mother doll out and studied her closely. Whoever had carved and painted the wooden figure had done an expert job. The green eyes seemed almost alive, watching Katie, and the lady's expression was so sad, it made her feel sad, too. Gently, she set the doll back exactly where she had been, staring at what Katie thought of as the little girl's room.

Next, she lifted the man doll, still in sitting position, out of his chair. The painted corners of his mouth were turned down as if he, too, was very sad. She put him back. Then she began pulling out things, admiring how the drawers on a miniature bureau really opened, the shelves of the china cabinet held cups and plates, and tiny books could be taken one by one from the bookcase. Clearly a great deal of work had gone into making the dollhouse. She was just reaching to open the wardrobe in the girl's bedroom when she saw a small patch of pale light beside the cabinet.

It was only about two inches high, and the brightness seemed to fade in and out, like a bulb about to burn out. Before Katie was sure she'd seen it, it flickered out. But, a moment later, she spotted it near the mother doll in the hall outside. A moment later, it winked out again, only to reappear in the den beside the chair where the father sat reading. Hardly thinking, Katie stretched a finger to touch the oval of light, but it vanished for good.

Very strange, Katie told herself. She sat still for a long time, as if the thing were shy like a hummingbird that would fly off at the slightest movement. But it didn't return, and Katie didn't wait very long. She was making her visits to the basement short, so that no one else would start to wonder about longer absences. This was all part of her plan to keep the dollhouse secret.

Two days later, the light was back, flickering from one dollhouse room to another. It moved so quickly, and faded so often, Katie sometimes couldn't be sure it was there at all. Then there were moments when it stayed put just long enough for her to study it. At times she saw the hint of a shadow within the little oval of light that reminded her of the time Mrs. Waxman, her first-grade teacher, had brought an egg to school and held it up to a lightbulb so Katie and the rest of her class could see the shadowy shape of an unborn baby chick inside.

Dollhouse

The shadow inside the dollhouse light seemed, at first, to have no special shape. But, as Katie played at rearranging the furniture (though she was always careful to put everything back the way it had been before she covered up the dollhouse), she had more opportunity to study the tiny wonder. She had begun to think of it as a ghost perfectly suited to the dollhouse. She also started to consider if Nana's story of the doll's ghost might be true. Like a shy animal, the ghost light seemed to get used to Kate and would linger longer near her hand before flashing away to some other room. Over the next two weeks, she became sure she could see the shape of someone—a child—inside. She grew certain that she was looking at the shadowy outline of a child's head, a body, two arms, and two legs.

Her desire to keep the dollhouse secret let her slip downstairs only when the other family members were involved in their own business and not paying attention to her. Now she was also concerned that anyone else might scare away the light once and for all and undo Katie's patient efforts to make friends.

She still had to push through the invisible wall. It was soft, stubborn, but always, in the end, allowed her to reach into the rooms it guarded. Though the ghost appeared more comfortable with her exploring hand, it never quite permitted Katie to touch it, though she felt that sometimes it was teasing her, staying just an inch or two away from her fingertips as if daring her to touch. But when Katie tried, it blinked out and turned up in another corner.

Then, near the end of the second week, came the moment when Katie moved her finger quickly as the "ghost" drew tantalizingly near. For an instant, she felt something like an electric shock race down her finger, through her hand, and up her arm, almost to the elbow. It felt like the jolt when she hit her funny bone, not nice at all. Her finger numbed, while the rest of her hand and her lower arm had pins-and-needles prickles for almost five minutes. She was just about to go looking for her mother when the sensations faded away.

After this, she didn't see the little light again; she was afraid the ghost had disappeared completely. So it no longer seemed important that it was becoming harder to keep the dollhouse hidden.

Things were pretty settled on the upstairs floors. There were still lots of little jobs to do, and Katie was expected to pitch in sweeping and dusting and so on. When she could sneak down to the basement, she found herself growing bored with the toy house. She had tired of moving the furniture around. She never saw the ghost anymore. She wondered if she had scared it away—or even killed it. *But how can you kill a ghost?* she thought. *That makes no sense. A ghost is dead already.*

One afternoon she took a really close look at the base on which the dollhouse sat: a rectangle four or five inches high, covered with green felt that looked like a lawn. At the back she noticed two shallow drawers, also felt-covered, with only a faint crack, no bigger than a hair, outlining them.

With the tip of her nail, Katie pried them open. The drawer under the dining room held odd bits of tiny furniture: an end table, a chair missing a leg, a little throw rug rolled up and tied with a piece of string. She guessed these were items that had been replaced in the dollhouse but that some former owner couldn't bear to part with.

The second drawer was much more promising. There was an old black-and-white photograph turning yellow at the edges. It showed a man with a mustache and round glasses standing beside a pretty woman with long light-colored hair in an old-fashioned style. The girl felt certain it was red. Katie instantly recognized them as the painted dolls in the house. They stood behind a little girl who looked about Katie's age. She had long blond hair held in place with a pair of fancy combs, a lacy party dress with dangle ribbons at the waist, and gloves. She was holding a wide hat of some soft material with long silky ribbons at the back. It was hard to see the girl's face: Her eyes were scrunched up against the bright sun, and her face seemed to have been bleached by the light. She didn't look happy, though the man and woman—surely her parents—were both smiling. A breeze had blown the girl's skirt and her hair and hat ribbons into streamers. Something about that made Katie think of the picture of Pinkie in the miniature child's bedroom.

Under the photo was a book, bound in red leather and stamped with gold letters, JOURNAL OF MARIE CANTWELL, 1949.

Katie flipped through the first pages, but found them blank. Nothing had been written from January until June. Then, on June 21 of that year, she found the first entry. Someone, Katie was sure it was Marie Cantwell, had written:

I thought this journal a sweet but useless gift. Now I have need of it. Our beautiful Madeline— Maddie—has been taken to the hospital. A week ago, she was sick with fever. I wanted to take her to the hospital then, but Henry said it was just a passing thing such as all children get. Sometimes he thinks, because I came from France all those years ago, I make too much of things.

Dollhouse

But yesterday she had a stiff neck and back, then she began to have problems swallowing and even breathing. I write this in the hospital waiting for the doctor to tell us what is going on. It helps me keep my thoughts together. I fear it may be polio. It is always worse in the summer. I learned that our neighbor took several children, Maddie included, to the community pool. I had forbidden Maddie to go there, but she went with her friends. Such is the way with children. Here is the doctor. I am so very much afraid.

Fortunately, Marie had printed rather than using cursive, so Katie had a fairly easy time reading the sentences. She knew, from hearing adults talk, that polio had once been a big problem, but doctors now gave shots that kept people safe except in parts of the world where medicine cost too much.

After a break, the journal went on.

It is polio, the very worst kind. They are putting my darling in an iron lung to help her breathe. Oh! To see only her beautiful head on a pillow, and the rest of her, from the neck down, shut away in that ugly machine. She was awake. But

sometimes she just stares. Sometimes she
recognizes Henry and me. Then she begs us,
"Let me come home." I promise her that all will
be well and that she will be home in good time.
Henry says nothing, but his eyes are full of fear.

Katie rushed on past pages of Marie pouring out her
troubled heart to her journal. She was anxious to learn
what happened to Maddie. The writing became harder to
read; the entries would often start or stop in midsentence.
Then there was a break for several days. Finally, on July
13, Marie wrote:

Our baby is gone. Henry tries to be strong for
me. Family and friends try to comfort me. But
how am I to be comforted, when every waking
moment, and in every dream, I hear Maddie
calling, "Let me come home"?

Again, there was a series of blank pages. Then, for
August 29, Katie found a new entry. Marie's printing
looked less shaky. Her thoughts were clearer.

Henry would not approve. Today I had old Mrs.
Nabokov over for tea. She has Gypsy blood and

has special gifts. She confirms what Henry refuses to believe: that Maddie's spirit is lost, longing to come home. She tells me there is a way to call my darling back, so she can be with us in spirit. It means bringing together the person Maddie loved most—that would be her mother, me—and one thing Maddie loved above all others. That would be the dollhouse we had built for her for last Christmas. Oh! The way her eyes lit up when she uncovered it and found all the wonderful furniture and the painted figures of the three of us who inhabit it. It was too expensive, but to see her joy was to know that it was worth every cent. Since my girl is gone, I have put the house and figures in mourning. There is a secret ceremony Mrs. Nabokov will perform next week, when Henry is away on business. I cannot wait.

There were more pages of hopes, fears, prayers that the old woman's magic would work—that somehow Maddie's spirit would come home. She didn't understand: Shouldn't Maddie be an angel in heaven? But then, Katie never could quite figure out why some dead people went to heaven and some had to hang around as ghosts.

Then, on September 6, only a few lines:

I felt my Maddie. Mrs. Nabokov sensed her, too. But I cannot see her. I searched the house. I stayed for two hours in her bedroom after the old woman left. But Maddie did not come to me. Sometimes I feel she is very close, but she doesn't come. Why? Why?

Another long break. Katie was almost at the end of the journal before she found a December 12 entry, the last one in the journal.

The doctors assure me I will be fine. I do not trust them. They said my Maddie would recover, and we lost her. Henry has decided we will move. He has transferred to an office in another city. We have given away most of Maddie's things. I am too tired these days to argue. But we have agreed that we won't give away the dollhouse. Henry put it in storage in the basement when we sold the house. We will leave this bit of Maddie in the house. Perhaps it will bring joy to another child as it once brought joy to our darling. I leave this journal here, too, as a bit of my heart, *which you will always hold, my darling, until we meet again. But I will take the painted figure of you with me and keep it close forever.*

Closing the journal after reading those words, Katie felt very sad. *But the old lady's magic did work,* she thought. Somehow Maddie had come back—just not in the way her mother hoped. Her spirit had been caught in the dollhouse—maybe trapped forever, a tiny ghost endlessly wandering the four rooms of a toy world, imprisoned by wooden walls on three sides and the invisible fourth wall.

Aloud, Katie said, "You can't be happy in there. I wish there was a way to help you."

In the stillness of the basement, she was sure she heard a voice, no more than a whisper, beg, *Let me come home.* Then she blinked. The ghost was back in the pink bedroom where Katie had first seen her. And the shadow within the drop of light was clearly the shape of a girl in a flared party dress and a fancy hat. It drifted closer to the unseen wall, then stopped. To Katie, there came the image of a sad, tiny creature displayed in a glass-walled cage. But it was a person—or, at least, the soul of a person—held captive like a fish in an aquarium.

It's not fair, Katie thought. *There must be something I can do.* She was sure now that she was looking at the ghost of

Maddie Cantwell. If she just could get out of the dollhouse, she might be able to go on to heaven or wherever her mother was waiting. Katie was sure the ghost couldn't get out on its own, so she decided to help.

"Don't be afraid," she assured the diminutive blob of shadow-in-light. "Maybe I can lift you out. But you can't hurt me like you did before."

Let me come home, begged a tiny voice.

"First show me that you won't hurt me." Katie pushed against the airy wall with her finger. As always, it resisted, then gave, so her finger poked through near the ghost. This time the ghost light stayed where it was. After a moment, it drew closer to Katie's finger. "Show me you won't give me a shock," Katie insisted.

The light brushed her finger. This time she felt only a mild pressure, like two tiny hands caressing the tip of her finger. It was soft as the brush of a butterfly's wing when one had landed on the back of her hand. She tried to stroke the edge of the light just as gently, saying, "I must have scared you before. That's why you hurt me."

Two tiny branches of light—Maddie's arms—circled her finger. The ghost dipped closer to her skin. In a minute Katie planned to put through her whole hand, then wrap her fist protectively around the light, and (she hoped) pull it past the invisible prison wall.

Suddenly she felt a sharp pain, like a needle jab, in her fingertip. With a cry, Katie pulled her finger away. At that moment the ghost winked out.

The girl studied her finger. A tiny bead of blood had appeared; the whole of her fingertip felt like it was burning. She wiped the blood away and took a closer look at the little wound. It wasn't a round puncture like a pin might make, but a funny half-moon shape. Almost like a tiny bite. Had Maddie bitten her? Katie wondered. It certainly seemed so.

She wasted no time scrambling down off the plywood and hastily throwing the sheet over the dollhouse. She ran upstairs to show her mother, who asked, "Where did this happen?"

"In the basement," Katie answered. "I was reaching in somewhere, and it just happened."

"I told you not to play down there," her mother said, peering more closely. "It almost looks like a spider bite, but I'll bet you scraped it on something. I'm glad you had a tetanus shot a few weeks ago." Then she marched Katie to the upstairs bathroom, washed the finger, and put some ointment on it. "Now, go and play outside, and stay out of the basement."

The warning was unnecessary. Katie had no intention of going back there on her own. The dollhouse could stay covered up; Maddie could be alone, since she'd only been mean. Sooner or later her dad would clean out the basement and find the dollhouse, and then she'd have to warn him about it. But, for now, she just wanted to forget the whole thing.

But Katie couldn't forget. Her finger continued to hurt, even though the redness went away. She swore she could feel a line of fire, like a red-hot wire under her skin, creeping down her finger, across her palm, and starting up her arm. It kept her up at night. Her mother, alarmed by Katie's restlessness and complaints, took her to several doctors who could find nothing. The mark on her finger had vanished, but the hot wire kept moving farther up. When it reached her shoulder, it seemed to branch into two fiery lines, one moving toward her neck and head and one moving across her chest to her heart. Katie grew frantic. Her parents, convinced something was seriously wrong, though all the doctors and their tests assured them Katie was fine, finally arranged for her to stay in a hospital while endless tests were run.

With her mother and father on either side of the bed, Katie lay feeling too weak even to talk. The scalding wires had reached to her brain and heart. Katie felt like she was burning up with fever, stiff and sore all over. She could hardly bear to have anyone touch her. At times it felt hard to breathe or swallow. And when she dozed off, she had awful dreams. She was tiny and trapped in a giant dollhouse, had been for as long as she could remember, and had no hope of escape. The door wouldn't budge; the windows in the three walls wouldn't open; when she shoved and beat against the invisible fourth wall, it did no good at all. She was scared at first, then angry, and finally realized she would do anything—*anything*—to escape this nightmare prison.

More tests turned up nothing. "Let me come home," she begged her parents. "Soon," they promised. But Katie knew she wasn't going home. Something was very wrong. She no longer felt completely herself or alone in her body. It was like someone else was taking shape inside her. When she stretched her arm or shifted her leg, she was sure she felt someone else's arm or leg inside her own doing the same thing. When she tried to explain this, her parents and the doctors could make no sense of it. They just made soothing sounds and sighed and shook their heads.

Then unexpectedly she woke up one morning, seemingly cured. The fever was gone; she was able to breathe easily. Eagerly, she swallowed the soup, pudding, and ice cream that were brought her. She felt whole again, fine again, ready to be free again.

The doctors kept Katie two more days in the hospital before deciding there was no reason for her to stay any longer. She was wheeled out to the parking lot by a kind nurse, escorted by her mother and father. Her brother and sister waved eagerly to her from the back of the family van. In a short time, she was home again.

Her mother insisted she take a nap at first, though she wasn't tired at all. But she didn't argue.

When the house was quiet—her mother outside watering the garden, her father driving the older kids to a school soccer match—Katie slipped out of bed. She hurried to the basement, squeezed past the stacked boxes, and yanked the dust cover off the dollhouse. For a few minutes she just stared at it. Then she went behind it, poked her finger—the same one that had caused all the trouble—through the unseen wall. Next, using the fingers of her other hand, she pushed from the base of her finger down toward its tip, squeezing it like a toothpaste tube. When her tightening fingers had almost reached the nail, a little blob of light with a smear of shadow inside began to ooze from her fingertip. She squeezed with all her might. The blob became a glowing drop that suddenly dripped onto the floor of the miniature living room. Instantly, the girl pulled her finger free of the wall. In a minute, she had covered the dollhouse and was running upstairs.

She slammed the basement door just minutes before her mother came inside.

"Honey," the woman said, "you're supposed to be taking a nap."

"I couldn't sleep. Oh, Mommy, it's good to be home after so long."

"You *were* a long time in the hospital. But now you've come home."

"Yes!" said the girl, hugging her mother around her waist.

In the faint gray light under the dust cover, the drop of light rose from the floor and drifted across the hall into the room where the stiff figure of a man read a book eternally open to the same page. In the hall above, the figure of a woman in black endlessly stared at the open door of a little girl's room. From the wall, the image of a girl in an old-fashioned bonnet, her hair and hat ribbons forever blowing in a long-departed breeze, gazed back. None of the painted eyes noticed the tiny bit of brightness and shadow that now flashed hopelessly from room to room.

Tea House

Most of Larry Hamada's friends found the deserted *chashitsu*, tea house, frightening—even in sunlight. But the boy only found it forlorn and sad. It stood in a corner of McClendon Park in the center of Harrisport, Oregon, on the coast between Newport and Union City. At one time, the building had been the heart of the Japanese-American community there. Modeled after a famous tea house in Tokyo, it was called, simply, Cherry Tree Tea House.

Though it had been built to serve the Japanese-American population, it quickly became popular with the rest of the community and then with tourists. The owners, Mr. and Mrs. Jirohei, for years had owned a nursery and bulb farm in eastern Oregon, where they raised tulips, daffodils, and gladioli. When running the farm became too much, they sold the business and moved to Harrisport, where Mr. Jirohei had been born. There they achieved a special dream of theirs, building and running the tea house in the municipal park, with the blessing of the city government.

Willows shaded the creek that flowed behind it. Stone lanterns along the water's edge were lighted each night, inviting couples to stroll in the soft glow. In front was the cherry tree—now long since dead—that had given the tea house its name. Mr. Jirohei had imported the tree from Japan. It had been his pride and joy. He would sit playing his ancient bamboo flute under the lavish blossoms in spring or enjoying the shade it gave in summer.

Larry, who was also born in Harrisport, knew that the *sakura*, cherry tree, was an important symbol in Japan. The tree represented good fortune, love, affection, and spring— many positive elements. But it had other ideas associated with it. Because of the tree's short, intense blooming time, it was also seen as a reminder that life passes quickly. One bit of lore that an uncle of Larry's shared was that the cherry tree was once associated with samurai warriors. Their life was often fierce and glorious, but they could be cut down in battle at the height of their accomplishments. He claimed that a fallen samurai was often buried with only a cherry tree as a grave marker. So a cherry tree, in many minds, represented new life growing even in a place of death.

But something had happened in this peaceful setting eleven years before—by unfortunate chance, the year Larry was born. Mr. Jirohei had been killed in a holdup one night as the elderly couple was closing up shop for the day. By the time the police arrived, they found Mrs. Jirohei holding her husband's body. She could tell them nothing about the crime (which was still unsolved). Half mad with grief, she actually fought the police and medical workers to keep them from taking her from her husband's body.

Then she locked herself in the tea house that had been their shared love for so long. When the police forced their way inside, not a trace of the woman could be found. An exhaustive search of the park grounds revealed nothing. It was as if Mrs. Jirohei had vanished into thin air, or into the fabric of the tea house. The surviving family posted a reward, and the search continued for months, but nothing more was ever learned. In fact, the case became a classic "unsolved mystery" that was often mentioned on television shows or Web sites devoted to the strange, the occult, and the unexplained. Such things fascinated Larry, even though he rarely discovered fresh information about events at the tea house.

Yet the weirdness didn't stop with the woman's

vanishing. A cousin of the Jiroheis, who lived in San Francisco, inherited the tea house and the nearby apartment the old couple owned. He and his wife planned to reopen the tea house after doing some remodeling.

The venture was troubled from the start.

Workers' supplies vanished; a scaffold collapsed, badly injuring two men; a carpenter working late one night told of hearing strange sounds from *inside* the walls. He added that he was sure he glimpsed a human form crawling up the wall and across a ceiling "like a great big insect." Unwilling to stay, he had fled and refused to return except to reclaim his tools the next morning.

Word quickly got around that the place was haunted. It became harder for the new owners to find and keep new laborers, none of whom would stay after dark. But the work was finally completed.

Two days before the opening, the cousin ran a few errands and left his wife alone to finish some work in the new kitchen. When he returned, he found the woman collapsed on the floor. Medics replying to his 9-1-1 call pronounced her dead. It was rumored—one of those awful tales kids love to share—that she had a look of such terror on her face that it scared even the doctors.

After his wife's funeral, the man sold the apartment and

put the tea house on the market. But there were no takers. People shunned the place even in daylight. It was said it had somehow been cursed by the tragic loss of the original owners. People kept away from the place, as if the Jiro-heis' ill luck might rub off on them. The feeling seemed to be: Let it be swallowed by decay and weeds, taking what-ever bad energies lingered with it.

In time, the for sale signs were replaced with no trespass-ing warnings. To these were added danger signs. Shakes had fallen from the roof; much of the wooden decking was rot-ten and unsafe; weeds choked the gardens that Mrs. Jirohei had once lovingly tended. The old man's beloved cherry tree withered and died. Many said it had died of sadness, just like a person. Some late-evening passersby claimed to hear ghostly flute music on the breeze. One or two said they glimpsed the form of the elderly flutist, sitting on the roots of the tree, in the twilight. Now the city had reclaimed the property, though there were no plans to do anything with it.

Still, something drew Larry again and again to the old building. Part of it, he knew, was simply a young per-son's fascination with the mysterious and frightening—especially when such matters clearly unnerved his parents, who were visibly reluctant to answer his persistent questions about the tea house and what had (or might have) happened there.

Other adults he asked were just as reluctant to talk—though one old neighbor woman, who had come from Japan when she was just a girl, told him that she was sure the place was haunted by the spirit of Mrs. Jirohei. "Surely she died there," Mrs. Ozaki said. "And when people die troubled and grieving and angry, they become vengeful ghosts who will make all who encounter them suffer greatly. If the ghost is a woman, she is the most terrifying of all. Female ghosts are as relentless as the blade of a steel sword. Most horrible of all was the ghost of Oiwa. She never gave her faithless husband any peace. No matter where the man went, he would see her face in a paper lantern, her form in a folding screen, or her shape in a tangle of ivy vines. She finally drove him to madness and death."

Mrs. Ozaki's words gave Larry a fresh mix of the wondrous and fearful to ponder. But he gradually came to realize that if he was to find out the truth about the tea house—or some part of it, at any rate—he was going to have to find out for himself. Yet, as much as the mystery drew him, the old stories of shadows, strange shapes, curious lights, and eerie sounds that were repeated (mostly by kids) kept him from going too close to the tea house. He never attempted to go closer than the tipsy remains of a bamboo fence that was barely visible in the choking mass of rangy rhododendrons marking what was left of the once-charming gardens.

Even taunts and dares from his friends—with whom he had made the mistake of confiding his interest in the old place—couldn't nudge him to go.

It wasn't till he met Katsumi Takka, a transfer student from Seattle, that seeking answers became a possibility.

Kat and Larry complemented each other perfectly. He was overly cautious; she had a reckless streak. They liked the same Xbox games and scary movies; they disliked their seventh-grade English teacher, Mrs. Harper; edamame and sashimi; and Mimsy Lorimer and Tony Santucci—the class beauty and class bully.

"I've heard about the tea house," Kat said to him one day at recess when they were sitting beside each other. This was shortly after her arrival at Uchida Middle School. "What have you heard?"

By the time that the bell ending recess rang, he had told her everything he knew "for a fact," and a lot of things he had worked out on his own.

"Let's go look," she said, getting up from the bench. "I want to see for myself."

"Sure," he said, picking his words carefully. "Someday, yeah."

"Today."

He knew that they had plenty of time to catch a bus to McClendon Park for a quick view. It would still let him get home before his parents returned from their jobs that evening. But Kat's eagerness unbalanced him: He found he really didn't want to go.

"Uh . . . maybe it's not a good idea," he ventured. "I don't want to be late when my folks get home."

She wrinkled her nose at him. "You told me they're never home before six and don't even worry until seven."

"Yeah, but," he floundered, "what about your folks?"

"Aunt Ruth doesn't close her flower shop until seven. As long as I've got something on the stove when she gets home, she couldn't care less."

"Well, I guess—"

"*Done deal.* Now, move it or we'll be late for Spanish."

She set off at a run, and he could only try to catch up. All through the rest of their classes that afternoon, Larry had the feeling he'd agreed to something that wasn't a good choice. *Not a good choice at all,* some nagging little voice kept repeating at the back of his mind.

They had to ride partway to the park on the 24 bus,

which, two stops past where they got on, was taken over by kids from Frankel High School—shouting, shoving, screaming into cell phones, and generally driving adult riders to the front of the bus. Larry wanted to abandon their seat near the back and find room up front, but Kat said, "I like this seat. I'm not moving." Larry glanced around, fearful of a confrontation, but Kat held her ground and—short of appearing a supreme wuss—he had no choice but to sit firm, too. A couple of the older kids gave them looks; Kat just stared right back. Larry tried to keep his gaze steady, but he found himself repeatedly turning to look out the window or study the increasingly trash-strewn floor. Kat never wavered, regarding the older kids with a steady, almost adult distaste that deflected all high school challenges.

At Center Street, most of the older kids got off to catch crosstown buses. Larry and Kat rode the last half-dozen blocks to the park in peace.

It was nearing the end of a bright spring day—perfect for showing off the tea house in a way that suggested only sadness, but nothing scary. They stood just outside the waist-high bamboo gate that seemed held together by the no trespassing and danger signs nailed to it. The westering sun left pools of light around the shadows of the dried-up koi pond. One of the boys who had dared to explore the grounds after dark reported that you could see the bones of the fish that had been left to die when the tea house had been abandoned last time. He said they glowed in the moonlight.

Other kids suspected he was lying, but none had the nerve to check it out themselves. This was probably the start of the story that, at night, when there was a full moon, the empty pond would fill with moonglow, and you could see unearthly koi, faintly gold and white and silver, swimming in the thick light. Their scales and skin were so transparent that you could see the shadowy, delicate skeletons inside. Like many such stories, it was layered over in each retelling. Now the ghostly fish were said to have piranha-like jaws—lots of luck to anyone who reached down to touch the undead monstrosities.

But today there was nothing frightening about what could be seen of the garden and the cherry tree and the tea house behind its deeply shadowed porches. For this, Larry was both grateful and disappointed at the same time.

"Let's go inside," said Kat, rattling the gate, testing its resistance.

"I don't—" Larry started to protest.

"Hey! You kids. Get away from there, now!"

In tandem, the twosome swung their heads around to

confront a brown-clad park patrolman—well, woman, really—in her Smokey-the-Bear ranger hat.

"We were just looking," said Kat.

"Scoot!" said the patrolperson. "You could hurt yourselves."

Larry saw that Kat was about to answer back, so he grabbed her hand and yanked her away. "We should go home *now*," he hissed.

Kat gave him the sort of challenging look she'd given the high schoolers earlier, then she sighed exasperatedly and let him lead her away toward Ambrose Avenue. Larry was aware of the patrolperson's suspicious eyes boring holes into his back, and Kat's eyes drilling into the side of his head as he hustled her to the bus station.

Kat didn't say a word until they were seated on the bus swaying its way back toward home turf. Halfway there she said, in a soft voice that, nevertheless, told him there was no room for his wussy arguments, "We're going back—at night—to look inside."

Any arguments Larry might have made died in his throat, long before they reached his lips. The fierceness in Kat's eyes and the set line of her lips assured him that she would not pay attention to any argument he might muster.

Maybe she'll forget about it, he told himself. *Yeah, right*.

Tea House

It was only a matter of time, he realized, before they would be exploring the tea house by starlight and moonlight and flashlight.

But, for several days, Kat said nothing more about the place. The hateful Mrs. Harper piled on homework and subjected them to pop quiz after pop quiz—she was apparently panicked by the upcoming new state testing and the rapidly approaching end of the school year.

Larry had almost convinced himself Kat had forgotten completely when his cell rang on a Wednesday, while he was at the seventh level of Star Ranger X. He was tempted to ignore the call, but something in his head warned, *Don't you dare.* He froze the game and picked up the phone, instantly recognizing Kat's number.

"Hi," he said cautiously.

"We'll check out the tea house tomorrow night," she informed him straight out.

"My folks won't let me go out after dinner on a school night," he began.

"We're doing it *late*—after everyone is asleep."

"We can't get there at night—"

"I've checked the schedule. The 33 runs owl service all night long. It's slow, but it will get us close enough."

"I don't—"

"That is *not* an acceptable answer." Then (he could

envision the smirk on her face) she added, "Unless you are the *supreme wuss* of Uchida Middle School."

"I'm not—" But even as he said the words, he knew he would be if he chickened out at her challenge. After a moment, he conceded, "Where? When?"

"Tomorrow. The bus stop at your corner. One o'clock. Will your folks be asleep by then?"

"Oh, yeah—they're in bed by eleven."

"And my aunt never makes it all the way through the ten o'clock news. The bus goes by your corner at 1:07. Be there."

She hung up. Larry didn't like the idea—he was, in fact, frightened to death of probing the mystery of the tea house in the middle of the night. But he was even less inclined to appear weak and babyish in Kat's eyes.

So he hustled himself to the corner at the precise time she had decreed, his knapsack loaded with his father's heavy-duty flashlight, extra batteries, snacks, candles, and matches from the family emergency stash. Most important to him was the lucky *kaeru* charm—a small silver frog that his grandfather had given him. *Kaeru* was the Japanese word for "frog," but it also meant "to return." Travelers were supposed to carry the charm to ensure a safe return from a journey. His grandfather had given it to him when the family went on their first visit to Yosemite National

Park in California. Larry took it whenever he went on a trip. Tonight, having a little extra luck with him didn't seem a half-bad idea.

Kat was already waiting. She gave a sharp nod and then clutched his hand for a moment. Her grip was so tight, he wondered if she was having second thoughts. But he knew better than to voice his suspicion.

The driver glanced at the twosome as they showed their passes. For a moment, Larry was hopeful that he might question the two of them boarding so late and force them to abandon this middle-of-the-night adventure. But the man just shrugged and waved them on as they flashed their monthly passes. It was typical of most drivers these days, Larry knew: If passengers didn't make trouble, the driver wasn't about to hassle them. Increasingly unhappy, he followed Kat to an empty seat halfway down the aisle.

They exchanged only a couple of words during the ride out to the park. There were few owl-service passengers: a homeless man, who seemed to be riding just to have a place to escape the chill night air, and two women, chatting wearily, wearing matching uniforms with major hotel logos on the fronts of their dresses.

None paid the least attention to Kat and Larry.

At the park occasional hip-high lights provided half-hearted illumination on the path. The moon—nearly full—was far more helpful. Between the two light sources, they were able to follow the twisting path of stepping stones without much problem—pausing often, always on the alert for a late-duty patrol person or someone of more doubtful purpose prowling the darkened park.

Too soon for Larry's comfort, they reached the tea house grounds. The building, which was bathed in moonlight, appeared to Larry as both daylight harmless and midnight menacing. His best instincts screamed, *Cut and run*, but that would only confirm his wuss status to Kat.

At the rickety gate, with its warning signs, he hesitated. Not Kat. She quickly climbed over. For a moment, Larry was afraid that her weight might collapse the flimsy, creaking barrier, but it held. She stood on the other side, impatiently waving for him to follow. Pushing aside his misgivings, he scaled the gate—though he managed to get his left foot momentarily caught between two of the bamboo uprights. He started to panic. His struggle to free himself nearly succeeded in knocking down a length of fence, until Kat ordered him to stay still while she worked him free. He was sweating in spite of the cool late-night air and breathing so fast he felt lightheaded.

"Get over it" was all Kat had to say, before she started up the weedy, zigzag path through the tea garden toward the dark hulk of the tea house.

Tea House

Angry at himself for letting her talk him into this crazy adventure—and doubly angry at appearing such a cowardly klutz—Larry followed.

Passing the dry fishpond, a pool of blackness though the moonlight was splashed brightly over the surrounding grass and weeds, the boy was sure he saw pale shapes curling and gliding in the shadows—*the ghost koi?* he wondered. He didn't pause to look closer. Kat was already starting up the front stairs of the tea house. The closer he came, the more he was aware of a *tuc-tuc-tuc* sound far louder and more disturbing than the familiar chirp of crickets and the hum of flying insects. *Beetles,* he assured himself. *Deathwatch beetles gutting the walls and window frames and roof of the abandoned place.* Left to themselves, they would bring the place down as effectively as a wrecking ball, he'd been told.

"They're locked," Kat said, keeping her voice low as she gestured toward the big double doors.

He couldn't help himself. "What did you expect?" he snapped. His frustration at this whole stupid adventure and the distressingly loud clicking of the beetles—*deathwatch* beetles—were getting to him. Quickly he pulled his *kaeru* charm out of his backpack and tucked it into his jeans pocket.

"No problemo." Kat pulled a small but efficient-looking

crowbar from her pink plastic Hello Kitty backpack. With the assurance of a practiced housebreaker, she inserted the chisel end of the tool into the crack where the double door panels joined, gave it a sudden jerk, and cried, "Ta-daa!" when the doors popped apart.

"Where'd you learn to do that?" asked Larry.

"TV shows," she said, replacing the crowbar and shouldering her backpack. "Let's go check out what's inside."

She left the doors propped open to allow moonlight to spill through. Additional light seeped through the loosely boarded windows. Larry pulled out his flashlight.

"We'll use yours for now," Kat said. "I'll keep mine for backup."

The beam of Larry's flashlight picked out scattered *tatami*, bamboo mats, covering the floor of a large area just inside the doors. Beyond was a long hall. Rooms of various sizes, with only shreds of doorway curtains, opened off both sides, letting a faint ghostly moonglow leak through. In some of the rooms low tables were scattered about on *tatami*. The damp, rotting rice straw smelled of mildew. Each room was really a small alcove—some holding wall scrolls, *kakemonos*, on which Larry could glimpse faint traces of calligraphy or brush painting. But the artwork was so blackened and rotted for the most part that it was impossible to guess what each had looked like when it was new.

The place was silent, except for the sound of their shoes on the squishy matting—and the sound of beetles in the woodwork, relentlessly destroying the place from the inside out. *Tuc-tuc-tuc.*

At the end of the hall was a large kitchen area. Here the beetles' clicking was—to Larry's ears—incredibly loud. Kat, pulling open the oven door of a big, old-fashioned stove, didn't seem to notice. The raw wood floors were swollen with damp and very uneven. There wasn't much else to see in the kitchen—just some shelving with a few filthy bowls and a rusty, Western-style teakettle missing its lid. A small door at the back, probably to a closet or cupboard, was swollen shut by the dampness, which seemed much worse on that side of the building.

The sound of the wood-boring beetles continued to grow in volume. Larry suddenly remembered a movie he'd seen at his friend David's house, where cockroaches swarmed out of the walls and heater vents and light fixtures to smother a guy in a whirring, chittering, gold-brown tidal wave. The scene had horrified him then; now just the memory made his skin crawl.

"Seen enough?" he asked Kat.

She closed the oven door and shrugged. "I guess."

"I wonder what really happened to old Mrs. Jirohei? I thought there might be a clue. But she just locked herself inside here and—*poof!*—no one ever saw her again."

"Unless the ghost stories you told me were true," said Kat. She was far more interested in testing the narrow, closed door in the back wall.

He shrugged. "People tell them like they're true. Who knows?" Then he asked, "What are you doing?"

"This is the only place we haven't looked," she replied, digging her fingernails into the crack between the door and the jamb.

The beetles were suddenly silent. The unexpected quiet startled Larry. Even Kat paused, her eyes raking the walls and ceiling, as if seeking a clue to the silence. Then, unable to spot anything, she returned her attention to the door, giving it a sharp yank.

"I don't think we should—"

"Well, *I* think we should. Give me a hand."

The rusted hinges gave under their joint tugging. They managed to pull the door a little way open. A smell—*horrible*—rushed out.

The door resisted a minute more and then popped all the way open, nearly throwing Kat onto her backside. Larry grabbed the girl, steadying her, but kept his eye on the pitch-black space Kat had revealed.

Something moved—pale, slithering—in the dark. Larry thought of the imagined ghost koi in the shadow-pool outside.

Kat pushed him away, clearly annoyed to have to rely on him for support. But he barely noticed as he shone his flashlight into the closet.

He could see the head, shoulders, and arms of a woman who was, impossibly, climbing up out of the solid floor like a swimmer emerging poolside. Her face was framed by black flowing hair; her eyes were red; her mouth twisted into a snarl. She was clad in a white kimono. When she opened her mouth as if to scream, all that came out was the hideous sound of deathwatch beetles amplified a thousand times.

Kat, her back to the closet, was searching for something she had in her backpack and was unaware of the thing that was trying to pull itself up and out of the floor. For the moment, the boards seemed to hold the form back like an insect in glue. Larry's head churned with ideas as he tried to imagine what elsewhere she was climbing out of—the past, another dimension, some underworld? Possibilities crowded into his mind from all he had learned from books, television, his computer, and talking to people like Mrs. Ozaki about such a nightmare visitation. The only thing Larry was sure of was that he was looking at

the ghost of Mrs. Jirohei. And she was one very scary spirit.

He made a strangulated sound and punched Kat's shoulder, forcing her to turn around.

"Hey," she cried, and then looked where her friend was pointing. "Oh." She stepped back, clutching Larry's wrist.

The ghostly figure had extracted herself up to her midriff. The remains of her white silk kimono clung to the figure like a diseased outer layer of skin.

Ikikikikikik, chittered the ghost. Its long, curved fingernails—claws, really—dug into the wooden floor, gaining purchase, allowing her to haul herself partway into the room while she struggled to free the lower part of her legs.

"We need to leave *now,*" said Larry, who'd finally found his voice. Kat, never releasing his wrist, just nodded, following as the boy backed away from the writhing figure that chattered and grabbed at them, then dug nails into the floor again, and, lurching forward, left only her ankles buried in the flooring.

Hauling Kat after him, Larry fled down the hall. He had the impression of strange glowing things moving in the tea rooms opening to the right and left off the passage. His only thought was to reach the doors and escape into the night beyond.

"Whoa!" cried Larry, stopping so suddenly that Kat, who was looking back into the darkened hall, slammed into him.

The front doors were closed.

"We left them open!" cried Kat. She shook free of Larry's hand and grabbed hold of the twin doorknobs, pulling with all her might. Neither of the doors budged.

"Let me help!" said Larry. He tugged at one side while Kat gave her full attention to the other. Nothing yielded.

Ikikikikikik, chattered the dark figure inching along the hall.

The *scrape-slide* sound of the body hauling itself through the shadows was totally unnerving. Larry and Kat tore more frantically at the doors.

"Use the crowbar!" Larry hissed.

"Oh, yeah," said Kat, whose self-assurance seemed to have melted away and taken some of her wits with it. She pulled out the tool—but found there was no longer space enough between the doors to insert the chisel blade. The thin opening between the matching doors seemed to have healed like cut flesh.

Ikikikikikik.

It was close, Larry realized. He yanked the crowbar from Kat's hands and began gouging the wood. Chips flew, but the wood resisted his desperate blows as if it were now made of material far harder than natural wood.

IKIKIKIKIKIK!

Kat was banging her fists against the wood.

"We've got to find another way," said Larry.

"Oh . . . ," said Kat, who had suddenly stopped pounding on the door.

Something in her voice compelled Larry to turn and look to where she was staring, letting his flashlight beam follow.

Kat was facing the darkened hall. At first he couldn't see anything. Then he followed her line of sight up.

The ghost—the nightmare version of Mrs. Jirohei—was crawling toward them *across the ceiling*, spiderlike. But her head was twisted around so that she was regarding them dead-on with her blazing red eyes as she scuttled across the sagging panels. Now one arm snaked down toward them. The fingers flexed. The claws glowed in the flashlight beam.

"Window!" he shouted. He pulled Kat toward the nearest one, where the still-intact rice-paper-covered glass revealed the boards beyond, moonlight gleaming between the warped slats.

IKIKIKIKIKIK—the spider ghost was above them now. Larry couldn't tell what that twisted face showed more of—hatred, rage, eagerness—but it frightened him beyond anything he'd felt before. Escape was now or never, he knew.

"Follow me," he shouted. He put his arms over his face, started running, and smashed into the window. There was a jolting pain in his left shoulder, which took most of the impact, then papered glass and boards exploded out onto the veranda, and Larry went sprawling on the deck amid debris, getting jabbed with nails and cut with glass fragments. Dazed and groaning, he twisted around to look at the window gap in the wall above him. A moment later Kat appeared in the space, scrabbling over the jagged remains of the window frame and barricading slats. She quickly worked herself partway over the sill, ignoring the splinter ends that snagged her clothes and dug into her stomach.

Larry, still shell-shocked, struggled uncertainly to his feet, stretching out his shaking arms toward Kat. He felt like he was moving in slow motion when all his nerves were shouting, *Haul it!* But he moved quickly enough when Kat screamed, "She's got me! By the ankles!" Kat began to squirm frantically. Larry grabbed her flailing wrists.

"It hurts!" Kat sobbed.

Still holding her wrists, Larry threw himself backward. Kat flew through the ruined window. An instant later, the ghost hopped froglike into the window frame, hands and feet bracing her crouching figure at the window's four corners, clearly unmindful of the glass and splinters. Hardly pausing, the horror leapt after the kids, who were already fleeing down the stepping-stone path.

Near the lifeless cherry tree, Larry snagged his foot on a displaced stepping stone, stumbled suddenly, and sprawled onto the ground. He bellowed as his chin struck another stone. For a moment he was too stunned to catch his breath or focus his eyes. His head just kept spinning.

IKIKIKIKIKIK.

He felt the woman creature spring onto his back, felt her claws dig into him. He saw Kat stop, stare, gasp, pick up a stone, and start forward, ready to do battle with the ghost, though raw terror flooded her eyes.

Then there was a sound, as if someone was playing a flute, from his left, where the dead cherry tree remained.

The talons digging into his side loosened mercifully.

The music played.

The weight lifted from Larry's back.

He raised his head. His blurred vision swam from triple, to double, to clear focus. But he wasn't quite sure he believed what he was seeing: an old man, in a shining white robe, playing a bamboo flute. He was seated on the roots of the cherry tree, which appeared to be in full bloom, the masses of blossoms shining pale pink in the moonlight.

But it must be true—clearly Kat was seeing it, too. She let the stone in her hand fall to the ground with a soft *tunk*.

As they both watched, the old man abruptly broke off his playing. He looked very unhappy—angry, even. He pointed the flute, as if it were a magician's wand, at the pursuing ghost.

The spirit woman was frozen in a half-crouch a few feet from Larry and Kat. Her eyes were fixed on the old man's face. Her head jerked from side to side in puzzlement, reminding Larry of a dog given two conflicting commands. She took a tentative step forward, but stopped when the old man gestured angrily with his flute.

A warm cherry-scented wind began to blow toward the woman from behind Larry and Kat. Abruptly, with the power of a gale, it picked up the woman, spun her around, and hurtled her through the now-windowless opening back into the darkened interior of the tea house.

The old man raised the flute to his lips and resumed his soft playing. He began to melt like mist into the air; in a moment, his music had faded, too.

"Is it over?" Kat asked, casting a nervous glance at the spot where the ghostly woman had been lost to sight. Nothing stirred in the empty window.

"I think we're safe now," said Larry. But he and Kat continued to hug each other as though it was the only way they could keep from shaking apart after all they'd witnessed.

"I thought they loved each other," Kat said suddenly. "That must have been Mr. Jirohei. And the ghost had to have been his wife."

Larry, digging deep into what he could know or guess, said thoughtfully, "Yes and no."

"I don't get it," said Kat, sounding more like her old self.

"Their real souls may be in heaven, or wherever," Larry said, recalling a discussion he had once heard on the Discovery Channel. "What we saw tonight was leftover anger and a need for revenge from her. And he was some kind of echo of his one-time love for this place. Maybe those are things that have no place in the next life. But hate and love are such different kinds of energy, I guess they cancel each other out. I think that's what just happened."

Kat gave him a long look. "You sure have a lot of strange ideas," she said. Then she smiled. "That's okay. I've got plenty of unusual ideas of my own."

Bone-weary, Larry turned toward the way out. "I just want to get home. I could sleep for a week," he said.

"A month for me," Kat agreed.

"I think—" He suddenly froze, his words chopped off in mid-thought, as a sound like a cross between a sigh and a moan reached his ears. Seeing Kat go rigid with tension, he knew she had heard it, too.

Together they turned and looked back at the tea house.

To their dismay, they saw a clutching hand, the fingers twitching like a knot of pale worms at the end of a skeletal arm, reach shakily over the windowsill from the darkness inside.

"She's not gone," croaked Kat.

"She's weak, but some part of her is still there," said Larry. Renewed fear hardened to a lump of ice in the pit of his stomach.

A second clutching hand gripped the sill. As if this was a signal, the two spun around and fled, hand-in-hand. Unhesitatingly, Larry kicked out the rotting gate, no longer caring who or what heard.

The park was unnaturally quiet around them. They ran faster, nearly losing balance in their haste. They didn't dare pause to catch their breath until they stood in the comforting glow of a streetlight outside the park entrance. To their mutual relief, a few moments later a bus came lumbering along.

With nervous glances toward the shadowed park, they clambered aboard, flashing their passes at the driver.

"You all right?" the man asked, genuinely concerned. "You look like you've seen a ghost."

To his surprise, the two burst out in hysterical laughter. They were still laughing when they took their seats.

"Kids," the driver muttered, shaking his head. "Everything's a laugh to them. Must be nice not to have any real worries."

He popped the bus into gear and pulled away from the curb, the sound of the engine muffling the nervous laughter from his only riders.

Dust Creatures

On a late afternoon in August, two girls, who would be entering fourth grade when school started later that month, strolled along the verge of Bauer Lane.

"I should be going home now," said the smaller girl, Erika Nordstrom, whose family had moved to the small Maine town of Morgan Grove only two weeks before. She was ignored by the taller girl, Abby Newsom, a naturally friendly person, who loved to meet new people. When the Nordstroms bought a house three doors down from hers, Abby was delighted to find that Erika, one of the five kids in the family, was her own age and would be enrolling in Hathaway Elementary, Abby's school. "We'll have Mrs. Ogilvy as teacher," Abby informed the newcomer. "My brother, Jay, had her two years ago and said she's great!" She had quickly taken Erika under her wing, showing her around, filling her in on the neighbors, and giving her a crash course in the town's history. It seemed the least she could do for her new best friend.

But Abby had saved the best surprise for last: the old, long-deserted Fanning place, which was reportedly haunted. The house fascinated and frightened the children of Morgan Grove. And this was the perfect time of day to check it out, she assured Erika. There were no cars on the quiet back road that twisted and turned away from the town; there wasn't anyone else in sight.

Erika, not at all sure she was up for this adventure, anxiously glanced at her watch. "I don't want to be late for dinner, and it's a long walk back."

"It's just around the next bend— Jack-T, no!" This last comment was directed at her little white-and-black Jack Russell terrier, who had suddenly veered to the right and was straining at his leash. All the time he kept up a frantic barking at something unseen in the grass berm that separated the tarmac from the dense mass of trees and brush that walled both sides of the road.

"What's there?" asked Erika anxiously. She had been born and raised in Boston; Morgan Grove was her first experience of small-town living. Abby was often amused at the other girl's worries about wild animals or bats with rabies or getting lost when Abby led them exploring in the woods around town. Her list of fears included snakes, falling rocks or branches, and crazy people living in back-country shacks just waiting to kidnap unwary children. "If half the things you were afraid of were real," Abby had teased her, "Morgan Grove would be a ghost town. It's only dangerous when people do stupid things, like Billy Noonan taking a double-dog dare and jumping off Hag's Rock into Witchy Pond. The rock and pond are called that because people said that in olden days witches built bonfires on top of the rock on Halloween to bring up the devil; later, they'd send him away by tossing the still-burning parts of their fire into the water below."

"What happened to Billy?"

"Oh, he belly flopped big time," Abby replied with a disgusted sound. "Knocked the air out of himself, so he couldn't breathe for a few seconds. He would have drowned if some of the bigger kids hadn't pulled him out." She didn't add that she had been one of the kids urging Billy to jump.

To ease her friend's jitters, Abby, tugging on the leash, said, "He probably smelled a rabbit." She gave the leash a final, impatient yank. Jack-T got the message. With a final sharp bark at the unseen whatever, he returned obediently to Abby's side and gazed up at her with what she called his I'm-so-cute expression. As usual, this prompted her forgiveness.

A minute later, they rounded a stand of trees that grew almost to the edge of Bauer Lane.

"Ta-da!" Abby trumpeted.

Jack-T added his own yip of support.

"It's only a wall," said Erika, disappointment and relief in her voice as she gazed at the stretch of crumbling brick higher than a man's head.

"You haven't seen anything yet," Abby promised. "Follow us," she added, since the terrier was pulling her forward, apparently just as eager to show off what lay ahead.

A little farther on, they reached a huge double gate; metal pickets topped with wicked-looking spikes looked like spears rising up from the fancy scrollwork at the bottom. It had been black once, but time had turned most of the gate rust-brown. One half was slightly ajar, but the weeds and grass growing to knee-height all around gave the impression that it hadn't been opened in years, maybe decades.

Beyond was a three-story mansion topped by a central tower with a single round window. The place was pretty much a ruin now. What little was left of the pale yellow paint was peeling off the gray wooden walls. There was a huge shadowed porch, its sagging roof supported by six pillars. All the windows were framed with fancy carving; the roof beams and corner posts were sculptured, too: The whole thing gave the impression of a huge wedding cake left too long in the wind and rain.

"So what do you think?" asked Abby. "Isn't it cool?"

"It's old. But it doesn't seem very scary," her friend said with a shrug. "Just sad."

"That's because you don't know about it," Abby said smugly. "At night, they say you can see spook lights all around the place. My cousin who's in high school said that once he and some friends were driving by at night, and they saw a weird, pale man—probably a ghost—holding on to the lightning rod at the top of the tower. He kept moving his arm, like he wanted them to come closer."

"Did they?"

"No way. People say the ghost is always trying to get kids onto the property, but any kid who was stupid enough to get too close to the house has disappeared."

"That really happened?"

"Lots of times," said Abby. "The stories have been around for ages."

Erika gazed at the house with new respect.

Abby, on a roll with her storytelling, continued, "The place was built a bazillion years ago by an old sailor named

Captain Fanning. They say he traveled all over the world when he was younger, to some really weird places. He was into black magic and junk, and learned a lot of secret stuff from guys like wizards and witch doctors and medicine men. He had three daughters. When he built the house here and settled down with his family, he taught those girls everything he'd learned. His wife died right after the house was finished." Abby dropped her voice and said, "They said he poisoned her because she tried to stop him from teaching the girls how to use magic." Her voice dropped again, so that Erika had to lean close to hear. "His wife called it 'the devil's work' and didn't want her children to have anything to do with such 'wickedness.'

"Anyhow, she didn't get her wish," Abby said offhandedly, letting her voice return to normal. "When she was dead, Captain Fanning used his powers to turn his daughters into witches. You see those windows?" She pointed to the double row of windows, mostly boarded up, that fronted the first and second stories of the building. They were all exactly alike: tall, narrow, and tapering at the tops to a point like an upside-down V. "Well, they were built like that so the three witches could fly in and out on their brooms without knocking off their witchy hats."

"That's silly," said Erika. "I think those are all made-up

stories and you're just trying to scare me. I've really got to go or my folks will have a cow." She started to walk away from the gate.

Abby sighed. Sometimes, there was no figuring out her newest friend. Erika could imagine snakes and bats and crazies, but she couldn't see the old house as the possible home of deliciously scary things, like witches and ghosts. She kept telling herself that she'd have a better grasp of Erika's thinking in time. Suddenly, she realized Erika was serious about heading for home.

"Hey, wait!" she cried, halting her friend's departure. "Don't go yet. We should watch for the spook lights, at least. I've heard this is the *absolute best* time to spot them." She grabbed hold of Erika's shoulder and tried to pull her back to the gate.

"I've got to leave now. If I'm late, I'll be grounded for a week!" Erika twisted free of Abby's grip.

At that moment, while Abby's attention was elsewhere, Jack-T, with the instinct for mischief that seems to go with the breed, suddenly jerked the end of his leash out of the girl's hand. An instant later, he squeezed through the gate opening and went charging up the weed-choked road that ended in a gravel loop in front of the ruin.

"Jack-T! *Bad dog,*" Abby shouted.

The dog turned to give her an I'm-so-cute look, then

continued racing up the road toward the looming house. To Abby, he was acting like something was calling him.

"I've got to get him," she said to Erika, who hadn't moved as she watched the terrier bound up the front steps to the gloomy porch and promptly disappear from view. Meanwhile, Abby tried to force her way through the gap in the gate, but what was barely wide enough for the dog was too narrow for his mistress. "Help me push the gate open," Abby ordered Erika.

"It's rusty and dirty and hasn't moved in ages," Erika protested. "I told you I've got to go home."

"You *have* to help. This is your fault," Abby insisted. She was never above getting her own way at times by any means, fair or foul. Even with someone she really, deep down liked and wanted as a friend. At the moment, guilt-tripping Erika seemed the best way to get the reluctant girl to go with her program. She also knew that she didn't want to face Fanning place alone.

"Why is it my fault?" Erika asked in puzzlement.

"You told me you wanted to see this place. Then you made me let loose of Jack-T's leash, and he got away. So if anything happens to him, you're the one to blame."

Abby's barrage of words confused Erika and then overwhelmed her. "I'll help with the gate," she snapped, adding sourly, "but that's all."

"Help me push," said Abby, ignoring the rest of Erika's statement.

Miraculously, though the hinges were rusted and the rangy weeds and grass blocked the gates, the two girls, straining against the ancient metal, managed to get it open. With a groan of the hinges and a tearing of clumped grasses, the gate yielded the precious extra inches needed for Abby to squeeze through. Erika was more concerned that rust had flaked off and stained her hands and shirt and jeans brown. "My mother is going to *kill* me," she said, still panting from the effort. "Okay. I'm going," she announced.

"No way!" Abby insisted. "Remember: This is your fault. And I need someone to help me find Jack-T." Both girls looked toward the house; there was no trace of the dog. "We've got to find him before the sun goes down, or else who knows what will happen to him—or us—if this place is really haunted like they say? If you leave now, you'll be responsible for what happens to my dog—and to *me*."

Erika wavered. She kept looking at the house, but with a respectful, almost uneasy expression on her face.

The lengthening shadows at day's end were really getting to her friend, Abby realized, as well as the old stories. *But then,* she thought, *I don't want to be here after dark, either.* Aloud, she said, "Don't just stand there. Get in here." She crooked her finger at Erika.

With a sigh of defeat, Erika slipped past the barrier. This was easier for her to do, since she was smaller and skinnier than her friend.

"Follow me and help me call for Jack-T," Abby ordered. She started toward the front porch where they had had their last glimpse of the terrier. The two kept calling his name, but there was no answering bark. It was as if he had vanished into the shadows. Abby couldn't stop herself from remembering those stories about kids who had disappeared inside the old Fanning place. *Were there pets that disappeared, too?* She wondered. She couldn't recall hearing anything about animals, still it seemed perfectly possible. That thought made her shiver, though the evening was warm.

The mystery of Jack-T's loss was solved in part when they climbed the short, broad flight of steps to the porch. It was shaded by an overhang supported by six pillars carved in a way that made Abby think of a picture she had seen at school of an old Greek temple. One of the twin front doors, its hinges the victim of wood rot and nor'easter storms, leaned backward. It hung dangerously loose; Abby thought a single good shove would force it all the way down. But the tilted door left a gap beneath it that would provide easy access to a Jack Russell. It looked generous enough to allow the girls to enter as well.

Abby bent down and yelled her dog's name into the

dark beyond the opening. She thought she had heard an answering *Yip!* That was enough for her. "He's inside. Let's go," she said, as she dropped to her hands and knees and began crawling through the gap. She was careful not to brush against the half-fallen door for fear it might come crashing onto her.

"Isn't this trespassing?" Erika asked worriedly.

"Who's going to complain?" Abby asked, pausing halfway inside to talk over her shoulder. "No one knows who owns this place. Let's just find Jack-T and get out of here before it really gets dark."

She crawled the rest of the way through. A moment later, Erika followed. Abby had the feeling she was going to have to make this all up to Erika big time if she wanted to keep her as a friend. But, right now, she had a more important concern. Where was her dog?

When they climbed to their feet and brushed the dust from their clothes, the two girls found themselves at the head of a long, dusty hallway. There was enough gray light filtering through the warped window boards and the grimy but uncovered fanlight over the front doors to let them see. Darkening open doorways lined either side of the hall.

Everything was coated with layers and layers of dust. In many places it had formed into clumps the size of small animals.

"They're like those bunches of dust you find under a couch or bed if you're a messy housecleaner," Erika said. "My mom calls them dust bunnies."

"Dust *kitties*," Abby replied. "My grandma always calls them that. Weird, though. I've heard them called dust ghosts before. I just can't remember who called them that."

"They're gross. This place is creepy. Let's find your dog and get out of here real fast."

It wasn't too hard to figure out where the dog had gone. His paw prints could be clearly seen in the dust, though these were largely wiped out by a wide, wavy trail that Abby instantly guessed marked the passage of Jack-T's leash whipping back and forth behind him as he charged. The trail led directly to a massive flight of steps at the far end of the hall. The staircase climbed sharply up to the deeper darkness above.

Unhesitatingly, Abby headed toward the bottom step.

"Are you going up there?" Erika asked, her voice little more than a whisper. Abby wondered if she was afraid that talking too loud might rouse a ghost or witch as the day grew later. But those old stories, even though they seemed more possible with each passing minute, were not enough to keep Abby from her goal of retrieving Jack-T.

"Yes, I'm going up there," Abby answered shortly.

"And if you're going to be such a coward, then stay down here. *But don't you dare leave,*" she warned as she started climbing the stairs, all the while calling for the dog.

After a brief hesitation, Erika followed. "Don't leave me alone," she said.

Following the marks of the dog's dust-displacing climb, the girls ascended the steps. Erika winced every time Abby shouted for her dog. It was clear she was afraid that such calling would raise whatever might haunt the crumbling house.

Most of the doors on the second floor were closed. Abby opened one far enough to see that it was a bedroom. There was a big old bed with a drooping canopy over it, mostly now just rags and tatters that stirred in the draft from the doorway where the girls stood. Across the twilit space, Abby saw herself reflected in the oval mirror above a dusty dressing table; a crack ran diagonally down the mirror, so she saw herself reflected in two pieces.

"Boo!" she said to her broken self. She began to giggle.

"Come on!" snapped Erika.

Jack-T's progress down the upper passage had cleared a path through the dust, which seemed much heavier here than downstairs. The curling gray stuff would reach Abby's ankles if she stood where it was densest. In many places, it was extra-deep; the girl suspected air currents had created eddies that mounded the dust into rounded shapes in these spots.

"They look like little graves," Abby commented. "It kind of reminds me of a dusty graveyard."

"Please don't talk like that," said Erika, sounding on the verge of tears.

But there was no stopping Abby, who was following a train of thought now. "When I was really little—in second grade—some other kids and I made an animal graveyard. We buried everything in a patch of ground near a real cemetery: Cassie's rabbit, three of Todd's goldfish. We had a special ceremony for Maggie's hamster and someone else's cat—I don't remember whose. We'd even go through garbage cans to find dead mice and slugs and snails. Sometimes they'd really smell."

"That is so gross. Please stop!"

"Anyhow, it all got plowed under by the gardener's tractor when he was clearing the weeds outside the fence. I hadn't remembered that until now."

"And I'm sorry you remembered it at all," said Erika unpleasantly.

They followed Jack-T's trail to a spot in front of a narrow open doorway near the far end of the hall. In the faint gray light inside, they saw a flight of high, steep stairs angling sharply upward.

"It must lead to an attic or something on the third floor. Maybe to that tower, too," said Abby.

The disturbed dust clearly showed that Jack-T had managed to scramble up these steps, too. Abby was puzzled. At home, the dog wasn't crazy about stairs, especially ones that would have challenged him as these clearly would. But there was no doubt that this was where he'd gone. She called hopefully to him, but she heard nothing back.

"Stay close," she said to Erika, gripping the girl's wrist and tugging her forward before the other could protest.

Pausing from time to time to call "Jack-T! Here, boy!" Abby started up the stairs. Erika, her wrist still circled by Abby's fingers, followed.

The stairs were steep—each was twice as high as a normal step. To Abby, ascending them was almost as hard as scaling the steps in the funhouse at Playland. The girls had to use the railing to pull themselves higher on the twisty staircase. The steps, like everything else, were coated in dust. They could see evidence of Jack-T's struggle to climb up. But there was nothing to indicate he had come down again. Abby was sure her dog was still in the attic.

The two paused when they reached the near dark at the top of the stairs. The space was easily as big as the house. Light came from two dirty windows, one at each end of the space that had slanted walls and looked like the inside of a giant tent. They were standing in the middle of a dense sea of dust, several inches deep, where boxes and trunks and pieces of furniture stuck up like islands in a gray sea. Abby kept hold of Erika's hand, partly to encourage her, partly to keep her from bolting.

But when she opened her mouth to call for her dog, Abby began to cough. "It's so dusty," she said, when the fit had passed.

Erika sneezed and nodded and sneezed again.

The silence of the space was discouraging and unnerving. Why wasn't the dog bounding over to her and barking his head off? Abby wondered.

The dog's prints and leash marks continued to the left. But here the leash had left only a line, not the wide wavy path it had downstairs. It was as though her pet had slowed down so the leash had no longer trailed him like the wake of a motorboat. Had something made him more cautious here?

She let go of Erika's wrist, but, a moment later, Erika slipped her hand into Abby's as they moved to follow the path the dog had cut through the cushion of dust. Abby was vaguely bothered by the fact that the two of them were holding hands like scared little children lost in the woods in a fairy tale. Still, she had to admit, it made her feel just a bit better. Erika really was a good friend, she reminded herself.

"Here, boy. Here, good dog," Abby kept repeating. But the silence was unbroken.

They were almost to the window at the attic's end when the dog's trail ended in a big circle of violently disturbed dust. The girls could see bare, sagging floorboards showing through dust curls. There was no sign of the terrier and yet no sign that he had gone any farther than the circle. The dust outside the circle was not disturbed at all. They looked back the way they had come: There was only the path they had made following Jack-T this far.

"It's like he got here and disappeared," Abby said in a whisper.

"Why are you whispering?" Erika wondered.

"Now I feel like something might be listening," the other said softly.

"What something?" Erika asked, dropping her voice to a whisper also. She held more tightly to Abby's hand. Her friend, meanwhile, was looking thoughtfully around the vast, shadowy space.

"What are you looking for?"

"I don't know," Abby admitted. "I just have this funny feeling that something is going to happen."

Then both girls saw them at the same time.

There were things stirring under the dust—moving toward them. Too scared to say anything, the two clutched hands and watched as a dozen shapes, each the size of a rabbit, crept through the dust. It was impossible to guess what was underneath the filthy gray mat that was thicker than the thickest carpeting Abby had ever seen.

"Dust bunnies," said Erika. She began to giggle in a high-pitched way that made Abby feel even more scared than she already was.

"Kitties," Abby said, and began to giggle herself, though nothing seemed a bit funny at the moment. Then a sudden chilling thought came to her. "I bet they got Jack-T." Her throat felt so dry, her voice so weak, she wasn't sure Erika had heard her.

But the other girl had. "Now they're after us!" she cried. "Shoo! Leave us alone!"

Whatever things were under the dust didn't shoo. They came closer. Watching them, Abby said, "I don't think there's anything under the dust. I think the *dust* is alive!" She had an awful vision of someone climbing the steps to the attic, seeing their footprints leading to a bigger circle in the dust, and no trace of the girls to be found anywhere.

Dust Creatures

Though Abby felt frozen in place with terror, her brain was racing a mile a minute. There was so much dust. Too much dust. She wondered if the drifting-down everyday stuff that relentlessly covered flat surfaces and hid under couches and beds had been added to by other things. She imagined children or pets smothered by dust, crumbling away to become a part of the ever-growing gray carpet swarming with some bizarre kind of life. Maybe those stories of witches and magic in the early days of Fanning place weren't so far-fetched. Maybe what they were seeing was the result of some long-ago spell, or just some leftover magic lingering in the household dust, even after the ones who had conjured it had turned to dust themselves.

Erika was stamping her feet in front of the dust mounds, which had paused in their approach to the girls. Could her friend's movements actually *scare* such animated dreck? Abby wondered. She suddenly recalled a sick joke she had heard about a carpet layer who finished carpeting an old lady's living room. Turning to look over his handiwork, he discovered a single small bulge near the middle of the freshly laid carpet. Unwilling to undo his work to smooth things out, he quickly grabbed a hammer and pounded what he thought was an air bubble flat. To his surprise, it seemed more solid than he'd expected, but he finally flattened it to his satisfaction. The new carpeting looked wonderful. At that moment the old lady came into the room and asked him, "Have you seen my parakeet? He got out of his cage a little while ago." The workman shook his head, all the time looking at the newly flat spot in the middle of the rug.

"Step on them!" she told Erika. "Stomp them!" Abby brought her foot down on the mound nearest her, flattening it. A moment later, Erika flattened one on her own. But now they could see more and more of the rounded shapes swarming toward them.

Abby abandoned her plan of fighting back. "Run!" she shouted. Still holding Erika's hand, she half dragged her friend along after her. The sudden movement surprised the dust things. They froze in their circle as the two girls hurried between them, heading for the top of the stairs. Then there were hissing sounds as the dust things realized their prey might be escaping.

Looking back, the girls saw uncountable dusty shapes run together as they chased them. Now there was one big dust bulge hurrying toward the two of them. But Abby and Erika were almost to the head of the stairs.

Suddenly Erika cried, "Oh! It caught me. It hurts!"

Turning, Abby saw her friend frantically brushing at the gray mass that was creeping up her leg. Abby slapped at the thing, then dug her fingernails in and yanked it away from Erika's skin. It peeled off like a filthy bandage; where it had wrapped Erika's leg, the flesh was covered with red dots, like a thousand pinpricks.

Ignoring Erika's hurt, she hauled her the last few steps to the top of the stairs. Then they were pounding down the steps, trying not to stumble. Halfway down, Abby glanced up and saw what looked like a big gray wave—a dusty tsunami—gathering itself as it hovered over the staircase. Then it began to pour down the steps like a dry waterfall, adding the dust on the stairway to itself.

They reached the bottom, and Abby slammed the attic door.

A moment later, they heard what sounded like surge after surge of loudly hissing softness hit the other side of the door.

"Can it get out?" Erika asked fearfully.

"I'm not going to wait to see!" said Abby.

The two ran for their lives. Before they reached the top of the main staircase, they heard the attic door burst open. A boiling sound, like water dropped onto a super-hot griddle, seemed to fill the whole house.

On the ground floor, they rushed down the hallway, aware of the gray horror seething behind them. When they reached the broken front door, Abby, in a gallant gesture that surprised even her, told Erika, "You go first."

Erika needed no encouragement. She scrambled through the gap like a frightened mouse. A moment later, Abby was scuttling through. When they were both clear of the doorway, they looked back. Through the opening they could see a swirling mass of dust. But, for whatever reason—maybe the magic worked only in the house—the dust creature did not follow them out into the evening.

All the same, the girls hurried on until they had squeezed back through the gate. It was only then, as they stood catching their breath and trying to rid their mouths and noses and lungs of the lingering scratch and smell of dust, that the full impact of Jack-T's loss hit Abby. She began to shake all over and sob; Erika quietly hugged her and patted her on the back.

When the worst spasms of grief had passed, Abby impatiently wiped the tears from her cheeks. "We can't say anything about this to our folks, especially my mom and dad. They'd want to come right over and see for themselves. And that—dust monster—might get them. We probably shouldn't tell the other kids, either. That would only make them start to dare each other to check it out. I think it's better if we just don't tell anyone."

"But Jack-T is gone," said Erika, who had pretty well worked out the dog's fate for herself, it seemed.

"I'm going to tell them that he ran off chasing a rabbit

and I don't know what happened to him. You can say the same thing, if anybody asks you. And tell them it happened way back there, closer to town." Abby thought a moment and then added, "My parents keep telling me to stay away from the Fanning place. Of course, they're thinking how a kid could have an accident. They never think of ghosts—"

"Or *worse stuff*," Erika interrupted with a shudder.

"Or worse stuff," Abby agreed. "But kids have always known the place is haunted. When it comes to things like this, kids always know best."

"I guess we'll never find out what was up in the attic," said Erika. "But I read somewhere that witches had special pets, called familiars, like black cats and talking toads. Maybe what we saw was like the ghosts of those pets."

Abby shook her head. "I'm pretty sure there was just one thing in the end. But, who knows, maybe they were just killer dust kitties." In spite of everything, she began to laugh—a good laugh this time.

"Or *bunnies*," said Erika, beginning to laugh herself.

"Whatever. I only know they—or it—can have that old place all to themselves." Their laughter quieted in the evening stillness. Walking side by side, the two friends headed back down the road to home and never once looked back.

Many

"I found it in the attic," said Raymond, pulling a brown paper bag with something long and flat inside from his backpack. "It was with my grandmother's junk." He and his friends—Troy, Jerry, Sarah, and Mikal—were sitting in the sunlit backyard of Troy's house. The others crowded around as he unwrapped a bright-colored box.

"It's a game," Troy said, sounding disappointed.

"No way," Raymond insisted. "It's a Ouija board." He pronounced the word "wee-jah" and opened the box to reveal a folded board that did look like a game board. But when he unfolded it, they saw just a bunch of numbers, letters, and a few circled words scattered around. From the box he took a little piece of wood, shaped like a triangle, with small, stubby legs at each of the three corners. A circle of green felt was stuck to the bottom of each leg.

His friends peered closer.

"But what is it?" asked Mikal, whose voice always sounded whiny. "What does it do?" As he leaned closer, his glasses slid down his perpetually oily nose so he had to push them back into place.

"Don't you watch any scary movies?" Jerry asked. "A Ouija board lets you talk to ghosts and stuff."

"Like a cell phone?"

"You are *so* dense," Jerry said, "I can't believe it."

Before he could say anything more, Sarah said, "You put your fingers on the little pointy wooden thing—"

"A planchette," Raymond read off the box lid. He pronounced it "plan-shet."

"Uh-huh," Sarah said impatiently, "and then the spirits move it around the board to answer questions, yes or no, here"—she tapped the words, which were in circles in the upper corners of the board—"or it spells out answers in these letters or numbers." She pointed at the double row of letters—the whole alphabet—and the single row of numbers, from one to nine, then zero, below. There were also the words *hello* and *good-bye* in circles at the lower corners of the board.

"How do you know so much about it?" challenged Troy.

"I watched a show about real-life ghostbusters last year," Sarah explained. "It showed how these things work. These guys in this old house tried to get in touch with a ghost using one."

"Did they talk to a ghost?" wondered Mikal.

"I don't know. My mom made me shut the TV off and go to bed."

"Let's try it," Jerry said.

Sarah rolled her eyes at him. "You need to be in the right place. Someplace where there are ghosts. Your house isn't haunted, is it, Troy? Anyone die here?"

Troy shook his head fiercely. "No way. My folks wouldn't buy a haunted house."

"Raymond, your grandma died last year. Do you think her ghost is hanging around your house?" asked Sarah.

The boy made a face. "She died in the hospital. Anyway, she was too nice to haunt anybody."

"My hamster, Loopy, died last month," Sarah said. "Some people think that animals can come back as ghosts. Alicia Downey said her white rat came back as a little ball of white light that used to run around her bedroom."

"Get a grip," Raymond said. "First of all, everyone knows Alicia is nuts. And you want to call up the ghost of your *hamster*. Oo—ooo—oo—ooo! I am the ghost of Loopy. Booga-booga!" Raymond shook his hands at her.

Sarah giggled and pulled back, nearly falling off her seat on a low garden bench. "Okay," she admitted, "dumb idea."

"Besides," Mikal added, as if he was seriously considering the possibility of such a haunting, "hamsters can't spell, so we'd never get any answers to our questions from this *weejee* thing."

To his puzzlement, the others burst out laughing.

"What's so funny?" he asked.

Raymond always felt a little sorry for Mikal, who never seemed to get it. He said quickly, "We're laughing at ourselves because we were too dumb to figure that out for ourselves."

The others, following his lead, made an effort to stifle their laughter. They failed as a fresh round of guffaws erupted. This time Mikal laughed, too, though he still looked somewhat puzzled.

"So where *could* we test this thing?" Troy asked, serious again.

They were all silent for a few moments and then Jerry said, "How about that apartment house over on Seventeenth Street that burned two weeks ago? Two people on the first floor died there, and a fireman got killed."

"Perfect," said Raymond, quickly adding, "I don't mean that it's good anyone died—just that it could work."

"I went by the building a couple of days ago," said Sarah thoughtfully. "There's a big pile of burned wood and stuff out front, and the place still smells of smoke. You can even see some of that yellow police tape on the front door and other places. I got off my bike just to check it out, and I was just sitting there, looking, when this kid comes running down the alley, carrying a big old fancy clock with burns on it. He stopped when he saw me looking at the clock. 'What are you lookin' at?' he asked. Then he said, 'They're dead. They *sure* don't need any clock now.' After that, he ran off down the street. Anyhow, I figured he'd somehow gotten inside the place. Since there was no one else around, I pushed my bike down the alley and found out how he got in—"

"How?" the others asked.

"There's a piece of plywood over a back window that looks like it's nailed shut, but you can pull it back easily."

"Did you go in?" Troy wondered.

"No, I was afraid to leave my bike where kids were ripping off stuff. But I bet nothing has changed."

"Sounds good," Raymond pronounced. "Guys?" His friends all nodded, sealing the deal. Then Mikal said, as an afterthought, "Won't we be breaking the law? I mean, trespassing."

"It's not like we're going to hurt anything," said Raymond dismissively. "It's burned up anyway. The people won't care—like the kid said, they're dead. As long as we don't take anything, what's the problem?"

After a minute, Mikal nodded, though there was still a somewhat doubtful look on his face. But the others knew that, in the end, Mikal always wanted to be included in their group, so he'd go along with them sooner or later.

"When?" Jerry asked.

"Day after tomorrow—Saturday," said Raymond. "We'll tell everyone we're going to that matinee movie at the Plaza, *Puffed Up* or whatever the name is."

"Get the story straight," Sarah insisted (she always had a good head for details). "The movie is *Puffins on Parade*, and it's G-rated, so everyone's folks will be happy, and it's at the MetaPlex, not the AMC Plaza."

"Whatever," muttered Raymond, with a shrug.

"We can meet at twelve-thirty, right after lunch, at the corner of Seventeenth and Rosewood."

"But if anything goes wrong, we ditch," said Mikal.

"I think I got it," Jerry said. "Plan A: We get into the building and see what the Ouija can do. Plan B—"

"Ditch," said Mikal, folding his arms, pleased that he had contributed something useful.

"Okay," said Troy, "we're covered. We either dig up some spirits or we split."

Since it was now late on Thursday afternoon, the friends began to drift home: to dinner, to homework, to video games, or just to TV watching. Raymond was the last to leave, carefully repacking the Ouija box into the paper bag and replacing it in his knapsack.

"Think it'll work?" asked Troy. "That Ouija thing?"

"Maybe," Raymond answered. "My gran must have thought so; she hung on to it. I mean, what have we got to lose?"

"Nothing, I guess," said Troy. But, for just a minute, he seemed more uncertain than Mikal at his most doubtful.

With a shrug, Raymond stood, high-fiving his friend. "Saturday," he said.

"Saturday," Troy echoed as Raymond let himself out the backyard gate.

Not surprisingly, Mikal was the last to show up on Saturday. Raymond was just about to write him off when he came around the corner, frantically pedaling his bike. None of the others believed him when he said his dad had given him extra morning chores. They just looked at one another, sure that he had almost chickened out, until the fear of missing the adventure had made him decide to risk it.

"Let's push our bikes the rest of the way, so we can check out the 'hood, see if there could be any trouble from kids like the one Sarah saw."

The five walked along, making a show of chattering innocently, all the while keeping alert for police cars or meddling adults or older kids who might find it fun to intimidate a band of fourth-graders.

But the few people they passed paid them little or no attention. They reached the tall boarded-up two-story without a challenge.

Everyone stood for a moment, staring at the mound of junk in front of the deserted building: burned wood, a charred sofa, scorched mattresses, water-soaked books and clothes. It spilled off the sidewalk over the curb and into the gutter. In the still, cool air, the smell of burn and smoke was thick.

They took a last look up and down the street, freezing when one, two, three cars rolled by.

When the street was quiet again, Sarah said, "The alley is really deep—we can store our bikes way at the end. No one will see them in the shadows."

Single-file—Raymond at the front, Mikal at the rear—they steered their bikes down the alley. Luckily, the wall of the building facing the burned apartment house was windowless, so there was no chance of their being noticed by the neighbors.

They left their bikes propped up against some garbage cans and recycle bins, in an unlocked but fenced-in area at the back of the house. Raymond carefully removed the Ouija box from his backpack.

Sarah led the others to the window with the loose covering and signaled Raymond to help. The two pulled back the sheet of plywood, revealing a blackened window frame, empty except for a coat of glass dust on the window ledge, where heat had caused the paint to blister.

Jerking his head, Raymond urged Jerry to climb through. Awkwardly, with much grunting and groaning, the heavyset boy went through. Troy went next. Then Mikal, who managed to get a sliver of glass in his thumb and broke the rule of silence to yelp and announce he'd been seriously injured.

Raymond hissed at him, "Shut up or go home!" Mikal, waving his hand around, quieted down and scrambled the rest of the way through. With the others helping from inside, Sarah clambered through. Raymond passed the Ouija to her and then followed. They eased the plywood back into place as quietly as possible.

There was only minimal light in the little room they

found themselves in. It might have been a bedroom. But all the furnishings had been stripped out, so they couldn't be sure. The smell of burned wood was extremely thick: It seemed to catch in their throats. Mikal began to cough loudly.

"Knock it off," Raymond said impatiently.

Obediently, Mikal tried to muffle his coughing by clamping both hands over his mouth, but he continued to cough as they moved through the nearby rooms—guided by beams from the flashlights Sarah, Jerry, and Troy had brought. They crossed a kitchen, where a fire-blackened stove and refrigerator remained. Next they entered what must have been a dining room: There was a built-in cabinet, its glass-paned front cracked and smoked. Sarah couldn't resist pulling open one door. Inside were carefully stacked dishes, wineglasses, a china tea set—waiting for the owners who would never return. Sarah lifted out a dainty porcelain figurine of a ballerina, looked at it, then sighed and carefully replaced it. She secured the door before she followed the others into the big room beyond.

"Probably the living room," said Raymond, keeping his voice low.

There was an unburned chunk of carpet in one corner of the largish space. They could still make out a faint pattern on the well-worn floor covering. The smell of burning wasn't quite as bad here. There was even a faint draft blowing through the cracks in the plywood slabs covering the shattered picture window that had, in happier days, looked out on Seventeenth Street.

Raymond said, "This is perfect. Let's sit. Hey, Jerry— easy with the flashlight." His friend had been shining the beam over walls and ceiling, checking out the area. "We don't want to let people know what we're up to." Jerry dutifully snapped it off, since there was enough illumination from Sarah's and Troy's flashlights to see by.

"I used my computer to check out some things," said Sarah, as they sat in a circle and Raymond unfolded the board. He set the planchette on the center, its tip vaguely pointing toward the yes circle.

"This floor is gross," Mikal interrupted, wiping his hand on his jeans leg.

"Then stand up," Raymond snapped.

Mikal made a few more faces but stayed seated. His coughing had finally stopped.

"Do you mind if I finish?" asked Sarah, clearly annoyed. The others turned to look at her. "Anyhow, I read up on the fire here. The couple who lived here, the Crowleys—the ones who died—were kind of weird. Their neighbors said they weren't very friendly, and no one seems to know what kind of jobs they had. One woman said she'd seen Mrs.

Crowley buying black candles over at Hillcrest Mall." She paused dramatically.

The boys looked at each other. "So what?" said Mikal, confused.

"Black candles, devil worship, *duh*," she said, not looking directly at Mikal, whose face and ears burned red.

"And"—Sarah was clearly on a roll—"when I Googled 'Ouija board,' I found an entry—wait, I printed it out." She took a sheet of paper from her jacket pocket, unfolded it, and read, "Spirits with negative attitudes are the ones most likely to try and make contact through means like the Ouija board. The gravest danger is that it might attract the class of demons called 'soul snarers.' "

"That doesn't sound good," said Troy. "What is a soul snarer?"

"I'll tell you, if you let me." She continued reading, "Soul snarers catch the souls of people who have just died—before the soul crosses over to the proper place of the dead. These unfortunates become slaves for all eternity. The strongest of these demons"—here Sarah paused dramatically—"can even cause people to die before their heaven-appointed time."

"They can kill people," Mikal said. His voice sounded very small in the semidarkness.

The girl nodded. While the others sat staring at each

other, Sarah folded up the paper and tucked it back into her pocket.

"Are you trying to scare us?" asked Raymond, breaking the silence.

"I just thought it was interesting," Sarah said defensively.

"Yeah, okay," Raymond said. "If anyone wants to chicken out, now is the time."

No one made a move.

"Fine. Let's get going—we'll have to be heading home soon if we're going to use going to the movies as a cover story. So, everyone put a finger on the planchette."

All five did.

"Now what?" asked Troy.

"We ask questions," Raymond said. "I'll go first. Is anyone there?" he asked, speaking into the darkness that seemed to press in on all sides of their pool of light.

The planchette twitched.

"Stop moving it, Mikal," said Sarah. "It has to move by itself."

"I *wasn't* pushing it," Mikal whined.

Troy and Jerry swore they hadn't been up to anything either.

"Well, whoever's doing it, stop already," Sarah ordered, "or you can't be part of this." No one was clear exactly to whom she was speaking. "Is there anyone there?" she asked, repeating the earlier question.

This time the planchette jerked, then swerved to the yes.

"It isn't me," Mikal insisted, without being accused.

But the others paid no attention to him; their eyes were fixed on the little wooden triangle under their fingertips.

"How many of you are there?" Raymond spoke again.

The planchette moved to four letters, *M-A-N-Y*.

"How many?" Jerry asked.

M-A-N-Y.

"Are you ghosts?" Raymond took charge again.

The planchette was still a moment and then swerved to yes. Then it shifted across to no.

"I don't get it," said Troy.

"He—they—*whoever*—doesn't seem to know what it is," suggested Jerry. His voice sounded dry and nervous.

When Raymond asked the next question, he lowered his voice, as if it might offend whoever or whatever was working the board. "Are you the people who died here?"

"The answer was 'many.' But only two people died here," protested Jerry.

"Three—the fireman," said Sarah.

"That's still not enough to be many."

"Will you guys shut up?" Raymond snarled, and then added unnecessarily, "The planchette's not working now."

But they could all see that the wooden triangle was frozen in place, pointing at nothing in particular. Only Mikal had removed his finger.

"Geez, it's cold in here," he complained. He began massaging his upper arms. The others noticed the chill, too, but weren't really bothered by it. And, they knew, Mikal always had to have something to complain about.

"I think we need everyone's finger on the planchette, Mikal," said Sarah.

After pushing his eternally slipping glasses into place, the boy reluctantly placed his finger beside the others.

"Is it gone for good?" asked Troy. He was speaking only to the other kids, but the planchette suddenly veered to no.

"Are you—some of you—Tom and Geena Crowley? Those were the people who died," Sarah whispered to the others.

Yes.

"Who else is with you?"

M-A-N-Y.

"Are they ghosts, or what?" Sarah wondered aloud.

N-O-T D-E-A-D. N-O-T A-L-I-V-E.

"None of this makes any sense," said Jerry.

Many

"It's kind of like a riddle," said Troy. Then he suddenly called into the darkness, "Are you a vampire or a zombie?"

The planchette didn't move.

"You are so dumb," said Jerry. "You can see vampires or zombies. You can't see whatever's here."

"What are you, then?" asked Raymond, clearly tiring of the verbal runaround.

M-A-N-Y.

"I don't think whatever we're in touch with is the sharpest knife in the drawer," said Raymond, who had lowered his voice so the others could barely hear.

The planchette suddenly twitched and began swiveling back and forth across the Ouija board. Stopping to spell out the same word over and over: *MANYMANYMANYMANY.*

Mikal tried to pull up his finger, but it was stuck to the wooden triangle like it was superglued. The others tried to yank their fingers free, too, but the bit of wood held them fast.

"It's gone nuts," said Raymond.

"It's like my little sister's Talk to Me Teddy when something went wrong with the computer chip inside. It kept going, 'My-name-is-Teddy-my-name-is-Teddy-my-name-is-Teddy,' until my father tried to fix it and that was the end of Teddy." Sarah finished with a giggle that sounded more anxious than amused.

"Tell it to let go of my finger," said Mikal, sounding like he might cry. But the planchette, tugging their fingers, zigzagging back and forth, up and down, across the board, kept insisting, *MANYMANYMANYMANY.*

"Stop!" shouted Sarah, but the thing only moved faster.

"Make it stop!" Mikal screeched. He stood up suddenly, forcing the others to stand also. The planchette, removed from the board, twisted and turned like a living thing. "Ouch!" cried Mikal. "It hurt me where I cut myself earlier. *I'm bleeding.*"

Now the others could see some small smears of red on the planchette.

"Let go, let go, *let go,*" Mikal yelled. Then he batted at the planchette with his free hand. The thing flew across the room, disappearing into the darkness. They heard a soft *chunk* as it hit the far wall.

They were all pointing and staring at their freed fingertips.

"It took off some skin—just like Krazy Glue," said Sarah.

They had all lost a spot of skin, but only Mikal was bleeding. The gash in his finger seemed much worse now.

"I think," Raymond said dazedly, "I think we'd better just bag this and go home." The others could see that he was shaking, but they all felt just as jittery.

Many

Raymond leaned over as if to gather up the board, then had second thoughts and kicked it viciously into the outer dark. A moment later, the box followed.

"Let's go *now!*" he said.

They looked into one another's pale faces. Only Jerry had turned to glance at where the board had gotten to. Now he said in a strained voice, "Um—Houston, we have a problem."

The others turned to where he was pointing.

In the dark center of the room, faint shapes were taking form, like wisps of pale smoke hardening gradually into vaguely human shapes. The two nearest them were clearly a wild-eyed man and woman. Their skin and clothing were horribly burned.

"It's them, the Crowleys," said Sarah, her own voice getting shriller, as if she were bottling a scream. "I saw a photograph on the Internet."

"But who are the others?" asked Jerry. "They don't exactly look like people."

Behind the ghostly Crowleys, the glowing figures were tall, misshapen, showing a hand with too many fingers and what wasn't a foot, but a hoof, like on a goat or horse. "I think one of them has horns," said Troy, and he began to laugh in a really unnerving way.

"I think I get the 'Many' part of it—there must be

twenty or more," said Sarah, so softly the others could barely hear her.

"That guy with the burned uniform next to the Crowleys, he must be the fireman who died," added Raymond. "And none of them are really alive, but they're not dead and gone, either. That's why we were told they were alive and dead at the same time."

"And the . . . others?" asked Troy.

"Soul snarers," Sarah said. "They must have snagged the Crowleys and that other poor guy before they could get away."

Mikal, his voice flat, as if all the fear and complaint had been leached out of him, said, "I just remembered. From Bible class. There's a part where Jesus chases away a devil. And when he asks the devil his name, he says *Legion*."

"What are you telling us?" demanded Raymond, never taking his eyes off the silent figures.

" 'Legion' means 'many,' " said Mikal.

"And there are a lot of them," said Sarah. "I don't know what the Crowleys were doing when they died, but I guess they got way more than they bargained for."

The shapes were flickering now, like a TV screen when a satellite dish needs adjusting. The mouths of the three human figures were open in soundless screams. The vague shapes behind them laughed silently. It was like someone had pushed a mute button somewhere.

"Okay, okay, here's the plan," said Jerry. "Plan B: *Ditch!*"

They ran for the front door, praying that it wasn't nailed shut. Behind them, the room was suddenly filled with intense blue light that flickered and felt charged with electricity like the air during a thunderstorm. Above the crackling, they could now hear howls, shrieks, laughter. They didn't dare look back.

Troy was first to reach the door. He yanked on it. To their collective relief, it swung open, and they dashed through. A moment later the door slammed shut behind them.

They ran halfway down the block before they stopped to catch their breath and be sure no ghosts or demons had followed. None had. It was later than seemed right: Dusk had fallen. Headlights of cars passing in the street showed an empty stretch of sidewalk; a single cat glanced at them, then continued on its way.

"We made it!" gasped Raymond, who was leaning down, hands on knees, catching his breath.

"Where's Mikal?" Sarah asked. A quick glance around revealed only four frightened friends.

"He must still be in that place," Raymond answered in a worried voice. "We gotta go back."

Many

"No way!" said Troy.

Raymond glanced at Jerry, who said nothing, just backed away, shaking his head, palms out in a back-off gesture.

"Well, *I'm* going back," said Sarah. "Besides, all our bikes are there."

"You saw those . . . those . . . things!" Jerry said. "I'm not going back—at least not until the sun is up. Maybe not ever."

"We have to do something, tell someone, call the police," Sarah insisted. "You know Mikal. He could be scared to death, even if the things don't hurt him directly." She dug into her jacket pocket and pulled out her bright red cell phone. She punched 9-1-1.

Jerry made a grab for the phone, but Raymond held him back. The other boy complained, "She's calling the police. She's gonna get us all so busted." To Raymond, he sounded like a bigger whiner than Mikal had ever been.

"Don't you think Mikal is a little more important than whether you get grounded?" Raymond asked in disgust.

"I want to report a lost kid—well, not exactly lost, but he's in trouble." Sarah's words were tumbling out. The operator on the other end of the line had to keep asking her to slow down and talk clearly.

"I'm outta here," said Jerry, running off down the street, with Troy right behind.

"Jerks," muttered Raymond.

"The police are on their way," Sarah reported. "I said I'd meet them in front of the apartment and tell them what happened."

"*We'll* meet them," said Raymond, taking hold of his friend's hand.

"Mikal will be all right, won't he? I mean, if the police get him out fast?" asked Sarah, as they walked toward the burned-out building.

"Sure," Raymond promised in what he hoped was a convincing tone of voice. In the distance they could hear sirens racing closer.

But Mikal wasn't all right. The rescue workers wouldn't say anything to Sarah and Raymond, who were cross-questioned, then sent home in a police car. When their anxious parents learned what had happened, they were saddened and angry and threatened to ground the friends— "for this life and the next," was how Raymond's dad expressed it. No one believed anything about ghosts and demons. They thought the kids had been trying to scare each other and worked themselves into a panic that somehow cost Mikal his life.

Many

The newspapers reported the boy's heart had just stopped, since there were no marks on him except for a cut thumb.

"He died of fright," Sarah said positively to Raymond as they walked home from school. They'd become better friends. By unspoken agreement, they kept away from Jerry and Troy, who seemed just as eager to avoid them.

All their bikes were gone by the time a couple of parents volunteered to collect them from the alley. To Sarah and Raymond, this seemed a rough kind of justice, not worth complaining about. It was nothing compared to the guilt that didn't end with the idea of Mikal's death, but the horrible thought that he might now be a slave to the soul snarers.

It wasn't till much later that Sarah learned a final detail about what had happened that fatal night. She called Raymond, cell to cell, and when she was sure neither one could be overheard, she began, "Mona Greene's uncle is a police detective. I guess he worked on Mikal's case a little. Anyway, Mona happened to hear—"

"Yeah, right," sneered Raymond. "She's a snoop."

"Just *listen*, will you? When they found Mikal, he was lying facedown on the carpet. Somehow the Ouija board was under his hand—the hand with his cut thumb, remember?"

"Yeah, he made such a big deal out of a little scratch."

"It must have started bleeding again. Mona's uncle said there was a little blood on the Ouija board. It looked like Mikal was trying to send a message, and the only way he could do it was to circle letters on the board with the blood from his cut thumb. But he only circled four letters. Wanna guess what they were?"

"*M-A-N-Y.*" Raymond's voice was so faint, Sarah could barely hear what he was saying.

When she understood, she answered, "No."

"What four letters?" he asked, not really sure he wanted to know.

"*M-O-R-E,*" she said.

"Then it's true," Raymond said dully. "He's one more soul they've caught." He made a despairing sound. When he felt able to talk again, he found Sarah had already hung up. He kept the phone to his ear a minute more. A sudden, loud burst of static in his ear made him quickly disconnect. But before the sound was cut off, he thought he heard someone lost and crying, very far away.

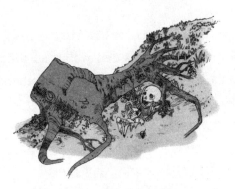

The Lodge

The hunting lodge was a lonely looking building, with the forest pressing in on all sides. The dark wood of the walls, rows of vacant windows, peeling paint on the shutters—it all gave Valerie the immediate sense that her father and two uncles had made a *BIG mistake* in choosing this Wisconsin site as the place for the annual family reunion and hunting trip. She'd heard Uncle Stu sing the praises of the place, where he'd gone with a bunch of his buddies the previous spring. The hunting had been good, and Stu couldn't wait to return. The prospect of good hunting made the place an easy sell to his brothers, Jim and Ed, Val's father. Their wives had been doubtful. Val's mother, Lynne, had argued for a return to the place on Little Bear Lake where they had stayed the year before.

But the hope of scoring a deer like Stu had bagged (the antlers, when mounted on his den wall, had prompted nods and even an admiring whistle from his brothers) had made it a done deal.

So here they were. Val could read big-time disappointment on her mother's face; her unhappiness was reflected in the faces of Aunt Mae and Aunt June.

Val climbed down from the SUV. Her older brother, Nate, who would be allowed to join the men for the first time this year, was all "Wow! This is great!"

It was Val's fourteen-year-old cousin Annabeth who put into words what she was thinking. "I can't believe it! This is the worst!"

"You'd better become a believer," said Mae, her mom. "We're in for the long haul." She handed her daughter a stack of bedding. "Let's get unpacked." Annabeth's discouraged sigh was loud enough to be heard all the way back to Madison. With a small sigh of her own, Val joined her family and relatives in moving suitcases and boxes into the lodge.

The inside, to Val's way of thinking, was no more promising than the exterior. The couches in the big living room sagged, the beds on the second floor were lumpy, the bathrooms needed immediate attention, and there were layers of dust and grime, complemented with spiderwebs *everywhere*. One day in this place seemed a stretch of the imagination; Valerie could hardly imagine a week.

It seemed a little better that night. The women collectively fixed a great meal of Aunt June's killer lasagna, plus salad and loads of garlic bread. It was all topped off with a plate of Lynne's lemon bars. Then the family adjourned to the living room, where the men—with much arguing and a lot of smoke—had finally got a decent blaze going in the fireplace.

Her smaller cousins roasted marshmallows and Val settled herself onto a couch, between Nate and Annabeth, while the men told stories and cracked jokes—some of the jokes cut short with a warning word from one or another of their wives.

At first the stories were recollections of past hunting or fishing trips—some quite funny, like when Ed had encountered a bear and the two had startled each other into running off in opposite directions. Annabeth rolled her eyes when her father, Jim, told for the umpteenth time about her near-fatal encounter with a rattlesnake on a forest trail. The three-year-old girl had thought the snake was a toy. She had been reaching for the hissing serpent, its rattles going full-tilt boogie, until her father, coming up the trail behind her, had stunned it with a hurled branch and yanked his daughter to safety.

It all created a comfortable, if slightly boring, atmosphere. Even Val was feeling lulled into a sense that things might turn out not so bad after all.

Then Stu said suddenly, "Didya know this place comes with a ghost?" Val instantly focused. Even Annabeth and Nate, teens who felt it was their duty to ignore most of their elders' stories, became attentive.

"Stu," June warned, "don't say anything that will give the kids nightmares."

Her husband made a face, but said nothing.

"Is it a true story, Uncle Stu?" Val wondered.

"Fella told it to me swears it was," said Stu, clearly relishing how all eyes—except for two of the smaller cousins who were wearing marshmallow noses and giggling—were on him, waiting eagerly for his account.

Smiling, Stu began. . . .

"Back in the 1920s this place was a private hunting lodge. Belonged to a rich family—their name was Swendson—who'd come up here for the hunting and just to get away. Like we're doin'! Sometimes they'd invite friends or relatives; sometimes it would just be the family and two, three servants—"

"Not a bad idea, a few servants," Val's mom interrupted.

"Hey, Lynne—let Stu finish, will ya?"

The Lodge

Valerie thought her father, Ed, sounded as eager to hear the story as Valerie.

"Anyhow," Stu continued, "one April, the family came up on its own—Dad, Mom, three older girls, and the baby of the family, four-year-old Alexander, his parents' darling.

"What happened was, on a morning soon after they had arrived, the girls went out for a walk. They hadn't wanted to take 'the baby' with them, but their mother insisted when little Alex—who apparently could be quite a handful—threw a royal tantrum because he wanted to go along. It seems whatever Alex wanted, Alex got.

"According to Martha, the oldest sister, they discovered a bird's nest or rabbit burrow—something with baby birds or animals—and were so busy checking it out, they didn't keep an eye on their brother, who wandered off. When they realized Alex was gone, the girls called and searched but couldn't find him. At last, when it was getting late, they hurried home and told their parents and the servants. The family searched until after sunset. When it seemed hopeless, Mr. Swendson drove into town and alerted the authorities. Led by the sheriff and his deputies, the townspeople of Westmont turned out in force to search for the missing child. But the search parties came up empty-handed. It was as if the boy had vanished from the face of the earth.

"All this time, the mother, Elizabeth, was growing more and more frantic. Days of searching turned into weeks, until, at last, the effort was called off. The conclusion was that the boy had fallen into one of the streams or into some sinkhole or simply that the remains had been carried off by a scavenger.

"The official verdict was 'death by misadventure.' To date, no trace of Alexander Swendson has been found. But his mother refused to give up the search. She stayed on long after the first snows began to fall. People in town would often hear her distant voice up the mountain, calling 'Al-ex-an-der.' Finally, when winter arrived in full and she refused to give up her searching, her husband had her taken away and placed in a mental institution. They say she'd sit day and night by an open window in her room, calling 'Al-ex-an-der' over and over.

"One night, she escaped. Folks in Westmont knew she'd returned, because they'd hear her heartbroken cries coming off the wooded slopes, calling over and over for her lost son. Search-and-rescue parties went out repeatedly, but they never got any closer than seeing a footprint in muddy ground or hearing her endless cries for her son." After a dramatic pause, she concluded, "They say that you can still hear her ghostly voice to this day. *Al-ex-an-der. Al-ex-an-der.*"

The Lodge

A silence fell over the room, broken only by the crackle of the fireplace logs, as all but the very youngest kids listened for a haunting cry.

"Booga-booga!" shouted Nate, causing the others to jump.

"Brat!" Annabeth laughed, slapping at him.

"That's enough ghost stories for one night," said Aunt June. "I think it's high time young folks were in bed."

Amid parental agreement and groans from the "young folks," the children—except for Annabeth and Nate—were hustled off to their assigned bedrooms on the second floor.

Val, who was sharing a small room with Annabeth, lay for a long time listening for a ghostly wail. But she heard only the distant hum of crickets or the soft *tunk-tank* of moths batting against the window screen. Then, as she was finally drifting off to sleep, she was sure she heard a faint call, "Al-ex-an-der," from high up the mountain. But sleep had too firm a grip on her; Val drifted off not sure if she had really heard a haunting cry or only imagined it.

The men and Nate left just before sunup, in quest of the perfect antlers. Val, still snuggling deep into the blankets to avoid the morning chill, heard the husbands reminding their wives not to let the kids go up the mountain, but to keep them close to the lodge. This, Val knew, was to avoid any hunting accidents—though the hunting party planned to go quite a ways into the woods in search of their quarry.

The kids were allowed to sleep in until seven-thirty, and then their mothers rousted them out of bed. Breakfast was a feast: orange juice, pancakes, bacon, hash browns, and a choice of maple, strawberry, or blueberry syrup. Annabeth and the older kids shot hoops in the basketball court they'd discovered behind the lodge; the littler kids found some board games in a living room closet and began a round of Uncle Wiggily under the direction of Aunt June, who kept saying, "This was one of my favorite games when I was a little girl." To Val, the board looked so old and grimy, she wondered if it had been tucked into the closet since the 1920s. *Had Alexander Swendson and his sisters played the selfsame game?* she wondered.

Not invited to join the older kids, not interested in playing with the younger ones, Val wandered off on her own.

"Stay close," her mother called through the kitchen window, where she and Aunt Mae were finishing the breakfast cleanup.

"I will," Val answered automatically. She had no plan in mind beyond simply wandering around to see what, if anything, the local area had to offer.

Remembering the rule to stay downslope, Val went

past the parked cars—two SUVs and a van—and followed the access road back toward the highway for a little bit. Then a trail suddenly veering off at a right angle to the road caught her attention. Feeling adventurous, she struck off into the trees.

The path ran straight for quite a while, and then it began to meander here and there and everywhere, as if it had forgotten whatever place it was trying to reach. At several points, it branched and then branched again. Val would turn this way or that, depending on pure whim, only avoiding those forks that unmistakably led upward. She was careful to heed her parents' warnings.

The air was heavy and warm. There were a lot of bugs, but the insect repellent her mother had insisted she wear seemed to be working okay. Val had no idea how long she'd been walking, since she had forgotten to wear the watch Uncle Jim and Aunt Mae had given her on her last birthday and her cell was back at the lodge recharging.

When she came to a clearing, she sat down on a hollow log to rest and to catch her breath. The day continued heating up. Val was sorry she hadn't brought a bottle of water or, better yet, Gatorade along with her. Her throat was beginning to feel dry and scratchy; her forehead and underarms and stomach felt sweat-sticky. She decided she'd have to head back shortly.

A rabbit hopped into the edge of the clearing, staring at her with a what-are-you-doing-here? look. Val froze to keep from startling the creature. It continued to study the girl for a moment—then hopped away as suddenly as if it had heard a gunshot.

It was so peaceful in the mingled sun and shade of the little glade, Val decided to sit and relax a minute more. She closed her eyes. The pine-scented warmth wrapped around her like a blanket; the hum of gnats and crickets was a lullaby inside and outside her head at the same time; she was adrift on a golden green sea, floating, floating. . . .

Suddenly Val jerked awake. The voice came: *Girl*. She was sure that the same word had roused her out of her doze. She glanced rapidly all around the clearing. Nothing.

Girl. It was a whisper in her ear—so close it seemed to tickle her lobe.

"Who's there?" she asked.

I knew once, this was a sigh, followed by a sad little, *I have forgotten.*

The voice was so faint, Val wasn't sure if it belonged to a shy child or a very soft-spoken woman. She remembered Stu's story from the evening before.

"Are you a ghost?" Val asked.

But the only answer was a wail, as if she'd upset whoever it was with her question.

The Lodge

"Sorry!" Val apologized hastily. "I didn't mean to make you feel bad."

The cry died away to a soft moan. Then silence.

Val stood up. She was half thinking that she was merely waking up from a vivid dream. She decided to begin retracing her path back to the lodge.

But she had barely taken a step when her right wrist was gripped—painfully—by the fingers of a smaller hand. Digits that felt like bones dug into her flesh. She couldn't see the ghostly fingers, but she could clearly see the indentations where her skin was held in the other's desperate grip.

Come with me, the voice without a mouth insisted.

"I can't. I've got to go home," Val pleaded, nearly frightened out of her wits, trying to pry loose the invisible, hurting fingers. But the other—whoever, *whatever* it was—wouldn't let go.

Please, the voice begged. Now Val was sure it was a young boy. *Come. I will show you what you must see.*

"I don't want to." Val felt disgusted at herself for whining like one of her youngest, brattiest cousins. Her plea was ignored. The unseen hand began tugging her across the clearing, then through the pathless underbrush into which the rabbit had bounded a short time ago. "There's no path. I'll get lost," Val protested.

But her captor only pulled her along more insistently. Slapping aside tangled undergrowth and low-hanging tree branches with her free hand, Val was helplessly drawn deeper into the wilderness.

She lost track of time. Heat, thirst, and weariness made her feel light-headed. From time to time she stumbled over tree roots or fallen branches or stones, but the hand just kept urging her forward—the circle of unseen fingers remained as tight and sturdy as a handcuff. She suffered one final stumble, but this time she sprawled full length on the leaf and pine needle carpet. At that instant the fingers let go.

Panting, shaking her head to clear it, Val clambered to her hands and knees. Not far from her was a fallen tree, its exposed roots facing her.

The light was dim this deep in the woods, but she could see something pale and yellowish white caught in the earth and rotted leaves clumped around the roots. Getting to her feet, she peered closer and saw there was a skeleton—a child's skeleton—so entwined with the roots they might have all been a part of the toppled tree. Fragments of moldy cloth stuck here and there to the ancient bones. Getting up more nerve, Val drew closer yet. Now she could see, around one wrist bone, a silver ID bracelet—turned black with the tarnish of age—on which she could just make out the initials A.S.

The Lodge

Alexander Swendson.

This was what the ghost wanted to show her. Val guessed that all those years ago, the lost child had huddled at the roots of the tree, trying to keep warm, waiting, praying for rescue that would never arrive. *What a sad, lonely thing to die out here so terribly alone,* Val thought.

"Are you still here?" she asked aloud.

There was no answer.

It was beginning to get dark. She hoped she could find her way back to the lodge all right, after being hauled through the pathless woods. She had no desire to share Alexander's fate.

Then she heard, far above her, the wail of *Al-ex-an-der.* There was no mistaking the call.

Bring her, the voice she now recognized as Alexander's whispered in her ear. It was so soft, she could barely be sure she'd heard it.

"I can't," she said. "I have to get home."

There was a heartbreaking sigh, then only silence and emptiness. Val was, she was sure, alone with the bones. The child's spirit had gone away.

The forlorn cry came again. *Al-ex-an-der.* It seemed a bit closer.

Val hesitated only a moment longer. Then she made up her mind and began pushing her way through the underbrush, up the slope toward the keening cry. It was hard to get a fix on the sound, which seemed to be now here, now there.

"Mrs. Swendson," she called, "I've found Alexander—ander ander ander. . . ." The name seemed to echo in fragments off the trees—maple, birch, pine, and more oak—that crowded closer together the higher up the slope she climbed. She was going in the direction her father and uncles had forbidden her to go—but she was sure the hunters would be well on their way home by now. They might also be hearing from her worried mother and aunts that she hadn't returned from her exploring. They might already be looking for her—in the wrong place. No matter. She'd worry about getting back when she'd finished the task that had been set for her.

It became harder to navigate between the trees. Briars and brambles and thorny vines snared her jeans legs. Still she struggled on, drawn by the sometimes near, sometimes far-off, cries of *Al-ex-an-der! Al-ex-an-der!*

It was getting harder to see. But Val was sure the last several cries were louder, nearer. Then she came unexpectedly on a forest pool, startling the young deer that was drinking there. As the creature bounded off, she called after it, "Don't go uphill. The hunters may still be there. Keep safe."

The Lodge

She tried to decide whether to go left or right, since the pool was fed by—and emptied back into—a swift-flowing creek, which looked too dangerous to cross.

Al-ex-an-der! The sound was so close it startled her, sending goose bumps up her spine.

On the other side of the pond, half hidden in the shadows of a cluster of birches, their pale trunks seeming to glow in the last light of day, was the luminous, transparent figure of a woman—or, at least, Val *thought* it was. She moved as close as she could to the water's edge, watching the shape that flickered unsteadily in the dwindling sunlight and deepening shadows.

Val edged closer; her eyes seemed to adjust more easily to the shifting patterns of light and dark. It may have been that the ghost—for what else could it be? she reasoned—was growing a bit more solid. Now she could clearly make out the form of a fairly young woman. As the image sharpened, it took on the black-and-white quality of an old photograph.

Val came so close the water in the pond lapped at her toes. From here she could make out that the other had on a shapeless black dress and some kind of black, beaded shawl. Her shoes looked sturdy and old-fashioned—like everything she wore.

Then the ghostly woman cupped her hands around her

mouth and shrilled, *Al-ex-an-der*. As close as she now was, Val felt the sound knife through her brain. She clapped her hands to her ears, but the woman's repeated cry sliced across her whole being just as fiercely.

"That hurts," Val protested. "Please stop." Then she yelled, "I know where your son is." She had no idea if the ghost woman could hear her, but she waved her arms and shouted, "Alexander is here."

The name stopped the ghost in mid-cry. The figure pressed her hand to her mouth. Val clearly heard a startled, *Oh!* The woman stared across the black pool at her. The girl felt almost chilled by the intensity of the look.

Suddenly, the ghost was striding toward her *across the water*; her feet hovered a few inches above the rippling surface. She moved less like a person walking and more like a series of quick cuts on a YouTube video—an unreal, jerking motion. The sudden onrush startled Val. She backed away from the water. Too late to run, she realized, as the ghost stepped onto the shore, and was standing in front of her, frighteningly close.

Alexander, the ghost said. The name was half a question, half a heartrending cry of pain.

Momentarily unable to speak, Val nodded.

The unearthly eyes, burning deep into Val's own, were filled with doubt and hope. The fierceness was unnerving.

"I'll . . . I'll show you," she finally managed to spit out.

When the other gave no sign of understanding, Val impulsively held out her hand to the woman. Elizabeth Swendson gazed down for a moment, then reached out and put her hand into Val's. The touch was no more substantial than a puff of air, but the cold was so deep, Val felt her fingers burning with it. Resolutely, she refused to let go. "I'll take you to Alexander," she gently reassured her companion.

The ghost followed Val silently as she threaded her way down the slope, trusting her instincts—and the occasional broken branch or crushed flowers or grasses she'd accidentally marked on her way up—to find their way back to Alexander's resting place. She didn't like to think what might happen if she couldn't find that spot again.

Soon, though, she was guiding the ghost woman along the side of the fallen oak. Now she was worried about how she might react to seeing the bones. *Will she suddenly lose it,* Val wondered, *and take it out on me?* Then the girl reassured herself, *You're not dealing with someone who's going to freak out in the face of death.* The thought struck her so funny she almost laughed out loud, though she realized there was probably more emotional upheaval than humor in her reaction.

The instant Elizabeth saw the bones, she gave a cry and

let go of Val's hand. The ghost sped to the tree roots. Val saw her trembling hand reach out for the yellowed bones, her fingers gently stroking the curve of the skull.

Alexander, she crooned. *Oh, my Alexander.*

She leaned over as if to cradle the bones, but somehow—like a magician's trick—she lifted out of the muddle of bones, roots, earth, and leaves the sleeping form of a young boy. She was crying as she pressed him to her heart. Val, standing now at a distance, saw the boy's eyes flutter open. Then his face lit up with joy, and he buried his face on his mother's shoulder.

An instant later, the vision was gone. Val was alone; only the bones caught in the roots remained as proof of what she'd witnessed.

"Be happy," Val whispered at last. Then, like someone waking from a dream, she looked around. Night had fallen. The branches of the trees pressed so close together, she could glimpse only a sliver or two of starry sky overhead. She had a vague sense of which way to head. But her gut told her she was in for a long, cold ordeal, trying to find her way through the now-ominous night woods.

And then, in front of her, silently radiating friendship and comfort, were two orbs, one large as a soccer ball and blue, one baseball-sized and yellow, floating in place, undisturbed by the night breezes. In wonder, Val took a step toward them, but they retreated a bit, and then paused. She quickly got the sense that they were waiting for her to follow. *Guides.*

As she trailed them through the night, they proved unerring—when they hovered in place, she looked around carefully and spotted a treacherous root, sinkhole, or other hazard. As soon as she'd negotiated the dangerous spot, they led her farther down the mountain.

Even when she recognized the path, they stayed with her, until she was standing on the gravel drive that led directly to the lodge.

Then they winked out, and she was alone in the night. "Thank you," she called.

A moment later, she saw flashlight beams stabbing through the dark. "Here she is!" Nate shouted. "I found Val." Then he muttered, "You're in deep doo-doo, Sis, scaring everyone like that."

But Val was feeling far too satisfied to do more than shrug as her family clustered around.

La Casa de las Muertas

The Garcia family stopped for lunch at a small taqueria just outside the town of Los Feliz. While their parents ate lunch under an umbrella, studying a fold-out map of New Mexico, at a second table Jose and his older sister, Isobel, bickered, which was their favorite thing to do. Jose made fun of Isobel's lunch of a tostada "without the taco shell, refried beans, guacamole, or sour cream," which were the best parts, in her brother's estimation. Isobel, who was rail-thin, seemed nuts to her brother. She accused him of "wearing more of his tacos than he ate." It was true, there was a dribble of salsa across his T-shirt, but he didn't care. The food was good, the patio sunny and warm, and the afternoon promised an interesting adventure, if their father, Diego Garcia, could figure out how to get to the remains of the hacienda where his grandmother—the famous painter Martina Garcia—had lived.

Jose had seen some of his great-grandmother's paintings in museums or reproduced as prints and postcards sold in cafés and gift shops. The family's most cherished possession was her painting of Taos Pueblo, the famous New Mexico landmark, that hung above the fireplace at their home in San Francisco's Mission District.

When he was little, Jose had not really been aware of his great-grandmother's fame. But during fifth grade she had been the subject of one of Ms. Coppersmith's classes. Jose even gave a report on his great-grandmother Martina and her art. Most of his information came from *The Art of Martina Garcia*, a book proudly displayed on the family coffee table, plus a few facts from Wikipedia. He admitted he didn't remember meeting her: She had come to his baptism in San Francisco—her only trip to California. Lost in her art, she had secluded herself in her house in the New Mexico desert, to which few were ever invited—and those were mostly artists and critics who formed an inner circle. Apparently, her only real companions were a houseful of cats and two female cousins—as old as their mistress—who were her housekeeper and maid. Increasingly, they became her only links to the outside world as she grew more reclusive—a word that made Jose think of brown recluse spiders, who lived in basements or under porches and whose bite was far more dangerous than a black widow's. As a youngster, he imagined his relative as a brown, spidery-limbed "recluse" creeping quietly through a hacienda where the sun was never permitted, attended by two "black widows" in human form.

Now, sitting on the patio, the childish idea came back to him, vivid and grotesque, coloring their trip (his father called it a "pilgrimage") to the house. When the old woman had died more than six years ago, she left the house and most of her money to her companions. The rest of the family got a painting each, which was how *Sunset at Taos Pueblo* wound up in the Garcia living room.

Jose's mother, Esperanza, was less than happy with the side trip. She had enjoyed the vacation in Santa Fe, had had a great time at the hotel and restaurants and shops, but she wanted to continue on to Los Angeles to see friends. The visit to Martina Garcia's hacienda was adding a day's driving to the trip.

But her husband was firm about it. "It's something the kids should see," he said stubbornly.

"We don't even know who owns the place. Your grandmother left it to her cousins, who had no children or other family that anyone knows of. They died less than a year after Martina, according to your brother, Hector. No one knows who inherited the place from them. What if it was sold? It may be private property we can't get near." She stopped, having used up all her protestations.

"Then we'll find out when we get there," Diego persisted. "I'm not coming this far to turn back." He folded the map. "I've got the route in my mind. 'Kay, kids—let's hit the road," he called to Jose and Isobel. "And if you need a bathroom break, now's the time to take it." Isobel rolled her eyes at this, causing Jose to say in a high-pitched voice, "Oh, I'm in *high school* now—I don't go potty anymore."

"Shut up!" his sister yelled.

"Knock it off, the both of you," Esperanza snapped. The children had sense enough to realize she was not a happy camper. They shut up.

The route, as Diego had plotted it, took them off the main highway onto a secondary road that wound through a couple of sun-splashed towns. These were all alike: little more than a few shops and homes of mostly adobe, glaring white-hot under the sun that blazed in a sky without a hint of cloud. Jose was getting bored with the unchanging desert scenery: endless stretches of sand dotted with tumbleweed, cacti, or the occasional creosote shrub, with a border of distant hazy, blue-purple mountains. Some of it reminded him of his grandmother's paintings, but all of it was growing tiresome.

He couldn't imagine crossing the flat, broiling expanse in anything other than the family Explorer with the air-conditioning cranked to the max. The adults were in one of their silent spaces, his dad staring straight ahead through the windshield, as though afraid of missing a sign or land-mark, his mom, her head leaning against the passenger window, listlessly watching the countryside roll by. Isobel had fallen asleep, iPod earbuds firmly in place. Jose gave up on the scenery and played his Xbox. He kept dozing off or spacing out so he never could get beyond the lowest level of Conquest.

Jose was half awake when the car slowed and his father pulled into the gas station that seemed to be the hub of a town that was nothing more than a wide spot in the road. The gas station, a Circle K Mart, and a few houses were pretty much all there was to the place.

Rubbing his eyes, Jose asked, "Are we there yet?"

"Close," said his dad.

When they pulled up to a gas pump, a crusty old guy in grease-stained overalls and an equally grimy brown shirt hobbled toward the car. He wore a fisherman's hat with flies hooked all around it. *Where are the fish?* wondered

Jose, peering at the sun-baked desert. *Or is it some kind of a wishing cap, 'cause he wishes he was somewhere, anywhere else, where he could fish?*

His dad lowered the driver's side window. "Fill 'er up," he said. The old guy started the pump, then came back to ask about checking water and oil. Diego agreed, but asked first, "This place called Sunset View? I didn't see a sign."

The fellow nodded his head. "Yep, that's us. The sign blew down last sandstorm. Nobody's got around to puttin' her back up."

"I'm looking for a house—La Casa de las Mujeres— it's supposed to be off Comistas Road. It isn't on the map, but I think it should be about here. . . ." He showed the attendant the unfolded map. "See where I've penciled in a line? Do you know?"

"Yeah, looks about right—just go maybe seven miles down the road and look for the turnoff on your left. Lucky you've got a sturdy car. The road ain't been repaired any-time recent. But why do you want to go there? The place is old and pretty run-down, from what I understand. Ain't no one lived there for years, not since the last gal who worked for the painter lady died."

"The artist was my grandmother—the kids' great-grandmother. I want to show them where she lived."

The man just shrugged and moved off to check the oil

and water. Diego glanced a last time at his map, then re-folded it and replaced it in the map pocket on his door.

"Seven miles—not far now," he announced, trying to sound enthusiastic. His wife continued to stare out the window. Isobel slept.

"That's great!" said Jose, feeling that someone owed his father at least a response. In truth, the only real enthusiasm he could muster was around the fact that the end of his immediate boredom was at hand. After this, the next stop was Los Angeles, with two days at Disneyland already planned.

When they'd left Sunset View, Jose's father kept a close watch on the odometer. The closer they got to the seven-mile mark, the more carefully he watched the left side of the road for a turn-off. But it was Jose who noticed what his father had missed—a hard-to-spot break in the tangle of brush and snarled tumbleweeds that lined both sides of the road.

"Pop! I think I see the road," he shouted.

His father hung a U-turn on the deserted two-lane road and started back. When he saw it, he grinned and said, "Good work, scout!"

Diego turned cautiously onto the road that was little more than a ribbon of gravel and dirt running deep into the waste of sand and weed.

"Careful!" warned Esperanza as the Explorer jounced

through one rut and then another. The jolting woke up Isobel, who demanded to know where they were, why her father was trying to kill them all, and how soon they'd get to a motel with a swimming pool. She pulled her earbuds free.

"Almost there," her father responded, dutifully slowing the car.

"Where's there?" Isobel whined.

"Your great-grandmother's home," said her mother, keeping her voice deliberately neutral.

"La Casa de las Mujeres," said Jose. "The House of Women. I guess that was a good name, since there were just three women living there all the time." He grinned. "When I gave my report, I said the name in Spanish, and then wrote it on the blackboard. Jim Tessler, who thinks he knows everything, said, 'That means House of the Dead.' He got *mujeres* and *muertas* totally mixed up."

"Who cares? Just so we get there soon," Isobel grumbled. "I need some serious pool time." She replaced her earbuds.

"I need some serious pool time," Jose echoed in a high-pitched trill, then added in his own voice, "What a pain!"

"Don't go there," his father warned.

Jose went back to his Xbox.

The road seemed to go on forever. Their slow rate of speed, given the deterioration of the road, made the journey interminable.

"My *abuela* sure valued her privacy," Jose's father muttered. It seemed that even Diego was starting to regret this silly "pilgrimage." While his mother and sister didn't seem to notice, Jose was aware that his father was pressing on the accelerator. They were really going fast, but Jose didn't care.

The Explorer jittered and bounced, tossing the passengers around in spite of the new set of shocks installed just for the trip. Jose watched for some sign of the place they were heading to, but the desert seemed endlessly empty in every direction. Jose was bored with Conquest and decided to pull one of the other games out of his backpack, which was resting right behind his seat in the luggage area. He unsnapped his seat belt and turned around, kneeling on the seat to reach into the pack. Unfortunately, his hand holding the Xbox caught the cord of Isobel's iPod, pulling her earbuds loose and waking her up.

"What are you doing, brat?" she demanded, elbowing him in the side.

He shoved back. "It was an accident, stupid!"

"Don't you hit me!" She tried to smack him on the side of the head, but he had turned toward her, and her hand struck a stinging blow on his nose, which promptly began to bleed.

"I'm bleeding!" he bellowed, holding on to his nose with one hand, flailing at his sister with his other.

"Knock it off!" their father roared, turning around to put an end to the argument.

At that moment, Esperanza screamed, "Diego! Watch out! *Slow down!*"

Jose had only a moment to lean forward and glance through the windshield past his parents' heads to where a small coyote was frozen in place in the middle of the road—one paw raised, disbelief in its eyes. Jose was aware of his mother clutching his father's arm in panic, his father jamming on the brakes, Isobel screaming as the car spun a full 360 degrees and then slammed into a huge rock. Jose, without his seat belt to anchor him, was launched out of the backseat into the windshield and unconsciousness.

For a time, there was nothing. Then, gradually, sensation returned. Jose drifted in a strange, impenetrable darkness lit by occasional waves of red and yellow light. Gradually the blackness faded to dark purple, then to a rich blue, and finally to a white-hot radiance.

To the boy's astonishment, he realized he was floating weightlessly in the sky above the desert, which continued to broil under the afternoon sun. The ripples of red and yellow broke into flashing points of brilliance that he now saw were the lights of emergency vehicles: two highway patrol cars, an ambulance, and a tow truck. They were parked along the road edge near the Explorer, miraculously upright, its front end accordioned against an outcropping of gray stone. The engine had been driven back into the passenger seats. Jose tried to groan when he recognized the family car, but no sound emerged. There was only stillness; what he watched below unfolded like an old silent movie.

Near the wrecked vehicle, several state troopers talked to a medic, while two other men in blue EMT uniforms were grimly loading three bulky, zippered bags of heavy black plastic into the back of the ambulance: smallest first, then the two bigger bundles. *Body bags*. Jose recognized them from TV crime shows like *CSI*. He began to tremble, realizing he was seeing the aftermath of the accident. Did that mean he was dead—a disembodied spirit floating in the air?

No! he wanted to cry aloud at everything he was seeing and experiencing. But although denial filled his brain and being, he wasn't able to force out a single sound. He continued to hover in a deadening silence that was syrup-thick around him and over everything.

Below, the last of the body bags was loaded. The medics closed the back, and all three piled into the ambulance. Soon it began to back away from the wreck, angled around, then set off down the road. Though the vehicle's warning lights continued to flash, the driver kept a modest pace: No need to rush if the only passengers were sealed in black plastic, headed for some hospital morgue.

With quick efficiency, the tow truck driver hitched up the back of the Explorer, which was upright and could still be moved. Away he went down the road, with the two patrol cars following.

Jose watched all of this as if he was watching some television show: It all seemed so unreal.

Am I dead? he asked himself over and over. And always his inner voice screamed, *No!* Each time he reminded himself, *I only saw* three *black bags, and there were* four *of us in the car. But, if I'm not dead, I must still be alive. So how can I be here, floating like dust on the breeze?*

And if there were only three body bags, had one been loaded in before he became aware of the ambulance? That had to be the case, because if someone was still alive, wouldn't the ambulance have been racing off to a hospital instead of traveling at a normal rate of speed?

He was still attempting to piece together an answer, when he suddenly felt heavy. Gravity began to tug him out of the sky. He was sinking more and more rapidly back toward the earth. Then everything became a blur of light and a sudden, deafening roar that seemed to split the heavens from horizon to horizon. He tried to cling to some shreds of consciousness, but in the last moment of his plunge earthward, he blacked out.

It was very late in the afternoon when Jose came to. He was lying on his back, his head in the shadow of a barrel cactus, the rest of his body sprawled in the hot sunshine. He could feel stones and bristles under him, as if he'd been carelessly tossed like an old rag doll onto the desert.

He sat up quickly and collapsed back down just as rapidly when his head blazed into agony and then began to spin like the car just before the accident. His memory of the accident triggered a flood of thoughts. *Emergency response vehicles. Three body bags. Drifting in a sunlit, silent sky.* Had he dreamed this troubling out-of-body vision? As he lay still, feeling stronger each minute, he recalled what he'd heard about near-death experiences, a subject that had intrigued him since his best friend, Arturo, had undergone serious heart surgery a year ago.

"I died, man! I died on that operating table," Arturo had told everyone. "I was floating up by those big old ceiling lights, and I saw all them doctors and nurses working on me on the operating table. And someone shouted, 'We're losing him!' They all started doing emergency stuff to me, but I didn't care: I was on my way up and out of there. It was like I was swallowed by that light and kept going higher. And, man, I really wanted to see what was up there." He shrugged. "Suddenly I heard someone saying, 'Stabilizing. He'll be okay.' Then I fell out of the light, down through the air, and right back into my own body."

After that, Jose learned everything he could about people who had come close to dying—or had really died for a minute when their hearts stopped, before they were brought back by medics—and what they had to report. He just never thought he would have such an experience firsthand.

He stayed as he was for a few minutes, while the rocking and rolling world around him slowly calmed. Then, very cautiously, he sat up. His head still throbbed. He held his hand to his right temple; it felt sticky and gritty. When he pulled back his fingers, they came away pink, flecked with sparkles, like diamonds. *Or windshield safety glass*. But he was fully conscious; he could move. He guessed his injuries weren't all that serious. He touched a finger to his nose and found there was just a crust of dried blood there; oddly enough, his nosebleed from Isobel's smack had stopped.

But where was he? Why wasn't the ambulance rushing him to a hospital as the only survivor? He was on his feet, wobbling a little, but feeling stronger and surer with each passing minute. He looked around. He seemed to be about twenty feet from the road. He pulled off his 49ers cap, which, miraculously, was still in place. Maybe it had helped protect him when he hit the windshield.

Why was he here? Where was here? And why was he alone, with no one helping? As far as he could see, the road was empty; there wasn't a trace of people or cars. Slowly, a frightening answer emerged: After the accident, he had simply wandered away from the wreck in a shocked daze and then collapsed. While the emergency operation was going on, none of the medics or troopers could have guessed that he was passed out not far from them.

In any event, Jose had to get away from the still-baking sun and find help soon. Every minute in the desert, he felt, left him at the mercy of coyotes or rattlesnakes or—creepiest of all—scorpions. Just the thought of these things made him hightail it for the safer road surface, where no critter could slither or pounce on him from under a shrub or rock.

Jose was a good fifty yards from the horribly familiar outcropping of rock. He'd apparently wandered across the road from the accident site. Without going too close, he could clearly see traces of the crash in the litter of glass and metal that sparkled in the sunlight.

With a heartfelt groan, he tried to accept, as much as his still-shocked condition would allow, the deaths of his parents and sister. He let the tears stream down his face, making little effort to wipe them away.

Get hold of yourself, he was sure he heard the voice of his father telling him, though there was no one to see. If he lost it now, Jose realized, he'd just become a delayed casualty. He would force himself to be strong.

For a moment, hope flared in his mind. *Maybe I'm dreaming,* he thought suddenly. *I'm still unconscious in the Explorer or in an ambulance or already in a hospital bed.* But his head ached. The dry, dusty air was scorching his eyes and throat; the late afternoon sun, while not as fierce as at noon, was still making him feel like one of his father's shrimp sizzling on their backyard grill. He dismissed this image of home as wishful thinking.

Everything boiled down to the urgent need to find people, shelter, and transportation. He didn't fancy being alone in the wild after dark. Desert nights could be freezing, and dangerous things came out to hunt after sunset.

He stood at the side of the road and tried to get his bearings. He still felt a little dizzy; it remained something of an effort to link one thought to another. Should he start hiking back to the main road? he wondered. Or did it make better sense to make his way toward La Casa de las Mujeres? The more he considered, the less certain he felt and the more his head ached. An empty road offered no clue to the best course of action; an indifferent desert equally provided no hint or guidepost, as it lay pale gold-brown in the thickening light of day, like a tawny ocean frozen in place.

He dug a quarter out of his pocket, deciding to use his father's method for decision making: *Heads, shoot for La Casa; tails, the main road*. He tossed the coin and intended to catch it and slap it down on the back of his hand, like his father did. But he missed it, and the coin hit the dusty road with a soft *thunk*.

For a minute, Jose lost sight of it altogether. He crouched down, searching, then brushed the dirt away to see that heads was faceup. *La Casa. Great-Grandmother's house.* Pocketing the coin, he set out in the westerly direction. He trudged along, losing track of time, only noticing that it was growing late when shadows deepened on the horizon. What looked like a flash of light caught his eye. Then it was gone. Then it was back. He guessed he was seeing a steady light source that was being obscured by some wind-stirred tree or shrub. Indeed, a breeze had been rising, seemingly encouraged by the sinking of the sun.

He was sure it was a house. Maybe the geezer at the gas station was wrong and someone was living there—maybe relations of the old women who had lived with Martina and worked for her. And if there was power, there might be a phone. Or surely someone would have a cell phone, at the least.

As he walked, Jose turned frequently to see if there were any cars coming down the road behind him. But the way remained empty in both directions. He trudged slowly on, unable to force his aching limbs to carry him forward any faster. At least the throb in his head didn't seem worse. But the pain in his heart from his terrible losses grew with each step. Still he urged himself on, determined not to surrender to the desert and despair.

Finally, he topped a low rise and saw the house. The adobe walls, painted soft pink, now looked almost orange in the fading sunlight. When he got a bit closer, he realized the light he was following was an old-fashioned kerosene lantern. He'd seen these when his family went camping. Was the power out in that house? Then he remembered, he had seen no power lines alongside the road—no telephone lines. That probably meant they used cell phones there (but how would they charge them without electricity?). Would they even have service in such an isolated spot? He decided they'd have to have a way to get into town. At the worst, they could take him back to Sunset View, where he could find real help.

The double doors—massive, wooden—were painted bright green and carved with the shapes of local blossoms, each in its own tidy square panel. The door handles were brass, twin circles of Aztec-looking serpents. Seeing no doorbell or knocker, Jose rapped on the right panel; when there was no immediate response, he knocked again, louder.

This time, the door opened inward with a faint creak of unoiled hinges. Jose came face-to-face with an old—*ancient*—woman, her leathery features a deep brown; creases half hid her probing black eyes. She held a candle with a hand cupped around it to protect the flame from the strengthening breeze. Her arms, bone thin, looked almost spiderish.

"*Si?* Who are you? Why have you come?" she asked in Spanish.

Jose could understand Spanish, but he didn't speak it all that well. He asked, "Do you speak English?" When she nodded, he explained, "There was a car accident. I was hurt. Everyone else is dead." He caught his breath when he said this last part, choking back a threatened fresh flood of tears.

Her face showed nothing. She simply asked again, "Who are you?"

"I am Jose Garcia. Martina Garcia was my great-grandmother."

Her watery eyes widened at his words.

A voice, high and frail, called from the room beyond. He couldn't make out what was said, only that it was clearly a question. The old woman turned to address the unseen person in rapid-fire Spanish, barely above a whisper. Jose couldn't grasp what she was saying.

Abruptly, she turned back to the boy. "Come inside," she said, in English. "The senora wishes to see you."

Jose followed her through a short entrance hall. She moved with a stiffness that was probably arthritis but reminded the boy of a spider's skittering movement. They passed under an archway on the right into a huge living room dominated by a massive fireplace decorated with brightly colored hand-painted tiles showing suns, moons, stars, trees, rivers, oceans, and so on. The wood for a big fire was laid in the fireplace but remained unlit. Heavy wrought-iron candlesticks on the mantel and candles in matching sconces around the walls cast flickering light over the two women seated in the room. One, taller, was sitting in a heavy lacquered wooden chair like a throne. *La reina*, thought Jose, remembering his Spanish for "the queen," since the word seemed so fitting. Her gray hair was pulled back into a tight bun; her black dress and severe

black shoes made the boy think of someone in mourning. She wore no jewelry. Her pale face looked heavily powdered, though a closer glance revealed it was only the fairness of her ancient skin.

She regarded Jose with an expression that was neither hostile nor friendly, merely interested. To her left, in a far smaller and simpler chair—so small that it could hardly contain her bulk—was a second woman dressed in black, her hair coiled in a braid on her head. Her wrinkled hands rested on the old, leather-bound book she held in her lap. *Was she reading aloud when I interrupted them?* Jose wondered. He was aware of the doorkeeper standing at the threshold of the room, watching.

In the uncertain light, the faces of the women seemed to melt and reconfigure. There was something vaguely familiar and yet disturbingly strange about the queenly one. Jose began to regret coming.

"Tell me your name, *niño*," the woman said, "and why you have come to our lonely house."

As quickly as he could, Jose answered her questions, pausing from time to time to let waves of sadness wash over him. The regal one murmured something to the heavyset woman, who left, then returned with a handkerchief she silently offered to Jose. He nodded his thanks, took it, and wiped his eyes. Silently, she closed the double doors of the room.

Already suspecting the answer, he asked, "Do you have a telephone?"

"I am afraid we do not. We are cut off from the world in here." At this, she gave a grin that chilled Jose. The other two women chuckled softly.

"I need to let someone know where I am," the boy insisted, growing a bit angry.

"Oh, they know what has become of you," the woman said, the ghost of a smile still remaining in place in spite of her restless features. Suddenly, she wasn't smiling anymore. Her voice sounded gentler. "Don't you recognize me, little one? Though it was many years ago when we met."

Jose shook his head in confusion.

She passed her hand, with its swollen knuckles, across her face. The confusing face dance stopped; her features settled into place.

Jose knew that face—not from his baptism, but from pictures the family had and that he had seen in the coffee-table book.

Martina Garcia, his *bisabuela*, great-grandmother.

He whispered her name, but the sound lodged in his throat. He couldn't be sure he'd said the words aloud.

He must have, though, because she nodded, then said, "I have been sent to take you with me."

"Who sent you? Where are you taking me?"

"All in good time." She stood up. "Give me your hand," she said, extending hers. "Carmella. Ana. We will leave now."

The two other women, one still holding the candle, one the book, stood beside their mistress, whose hand was extended toward Jose. "Come, come, *niño*, we have a great distance to cross."

But the boy was backing away. "You're dead. You're a ghost," he said.

She sighed and gestured impatiently for him to come to her.

"There are no such things as ghosts," he said, remembering his mother's comforting words when he had awakened, sweating and screaming, from a dream of being pursued through a forest by nightmarish figures.

Suddenly, he knew what was happening. These old women were *brujas*, witches, which he knew existed, as surely as ghosts did not. He had listened eagerly to the stories told by the woman in the hotel gift shop, when she had found him looking through a book he had pulled off the shelf: *Brujas of the West*.

"Oh, yes," she had assured him. "Witches are very real. This land is witch-haunted. One must always beware: They can take many shapes."

"*Brujas!*" he cried. The women looked astonished. He thought it was because he had guessed their secret. He pointed at the leader—"And you took the shape of my great-grandmother to confuse me!" He had the sudden, frightening impression of three spiders, gliding herky-jerky down the strands of a spiderweb toward a snared fly.

Then he was running away, slamming through the heavy doors, ignoring their cries of "*Espere!* Wait!"

He fled from the room, across the entranceway, then yanked open the outer door.

Night had fallen. The air was chill. The kerosene lantern, the beacon that pulled him into the witches' power, had been extinguished. There was only moonlight and starlight turning the road into a silver-and-shadows expanse.

He paused a moment to look back. The three women were standing on the porch now, watching, making no effort to follow him.

Before they could create some awful magic to snare him forever, Jose ran for his life, pounding down the road. From time to time, he looked behind him for signs of pursuit—even looked at the starry sky for dark shapes fluttering across the face of the moon in the form of bats or broom riders. But he saw nothing.

A stitch in his side made him stop to catch his breath and give his body a rest. But he allowed himself only the briefest pause, then he pushed on, not as rapidly, but managing to keep moving.

Jose raced on until he felt like he was running his feet off. The world was a blur around him, smeared by tears and distorted by the night. When he stopped for a moment, he found—astonishingly!—he had run so far he had reached the place where his family had died. Now the glass and metal bits glittered in the moonlight. Helplessly, he shouted, "Papa! Mama! Isobel!"

Silence. He called again but again there was no answer. Somewhere a coyote howled at the blazing moon.

Then he saw twin lights approaching. At first he panicked, thinking it signaled witchy pursuit. But he got hold of himself and realized these were headlights coming from the direction of the main road. He began running toward the lights, frantically waving his arms. Then he heard the reassuring sound of an engine. He stood by the side of the road, still waving.

A minute later, a battered old pickup truck came to a halt in a cloud of dust and a squeal of brakes.

He ran up, shouting, "Thanks for stopping."

From the open window of the cab, he could hear a woman's voice complaining, "Why'd you stop here? Nearly made me hit the dashboard."

"I thought I saw something in the road," a man's deep voice answered. He sounded puzzled.

"Well, there's sure as heck nothing out there," the woman said. "Now, get a move on. I want to see them ruins at night." Her voice suddenly became warm. "I hear the old place is romantic in the moonlight."

"Yeah, whatever you say," said the man. He was looking at Jose with a curious expression. He might as well have been looking right *through* the boy.

"I really do need help," Jose said, but he knew his voice was flat and empty and too soft to be heard. A moment later, he stood back as the driver restarted his engine, gunned it, and tore off down the road.

Jose watched the fast-disappearing red spots of the pickup's taillights.

"*Niño*," a voice whispered to him.

Turning, he saw three shadowy figures on the opposite side of the road—the tallest standing closest to him.

"*Bisabuela*," he said. It wasn't a question.

She nodded. This time he saw that her smile was warm, and when she held out her hand, he took it unhesitatingly. He had no desire to remain any longer. Somewhere, very near, his body lay hidden by the brush, where he had staggered, hovered for a time between life and death, then come to his final rest.

"Papa? My mother and sister?" Jose asked.

"Each of us walks our own road into eternity. But others serve as guides."

"Will I see them again?"

"Perhaps," Martina said. "Perhaps."

A moment later, the road and surrounding desert were empty, save for a single coyote trotting across the stretch of gravel to vanish into the brush.

Doghouse

The kids who knew eleven-year-old Blake Hudson thought that he was so smart, he bordered on weird. Still, the boy was never a showoff or a put-down, so they accepted him—though they were leery of someone who aced tests, who always had a correct answer for a teacher, and who read so much that his younger brother, five-year-old Jamie, feared his brother would "burn his brain up."

Blake also had an ability to see, hear, or sense things others couldn't. He could find lost things—from pens to pets—just by imagining where they'd gone. No one would play a card game with him because he always seemed to know ahead of time what cards others were holding; and when his best friend, John Brunsfeld, was hit by a car while riding his bike, Blake knew about it before anyone else, even before John's parents. Although Blake told the Brunsfelds that John would recover fully, they waited for the doctors to confirm this before they were reassured.

Gillian Dunlap informed Jamie, "Blake is an esperer." When Jamie asked "What's an esperer?" she replied, "He's got esp: He can see what isn't there. People with strange powers have esp. That's why they're called esperers."

When Jamie got home, he found Blake in his room, packing for their trip to visit their uncle. Blake looked at his brother and asked, "What's up, J?"

"What's esp?" the younger boy asked.

"Esp?" his brother made a face. "Never heard of it."

"Gillian says you've got so much esp, you're an esperer. She says you've got some kind of special brain power."

"Oh, *Gillian*," Blake said, wrinkling his nose. "She never gets anything right. "She's talking about ESP— extrasensory perception. You never call it esp, and esperer is out there—even for Gillian. Anyhow, ESP just means a special mind power that a few people are supposed to have that lets them see what most people can't, like junk that's lost or the future or maybe even ghosts. Sometimes they help police by touching something from where a crime has been committed that lets them see in their minds who did it. ESP works in lots of different ways. I guess you're either born with it or not."

"Were you born with it?"

Blake shrugged. "I don't know. Sometimes I think so."

"Like when you saw old lady Handley waving from her upstairs window two weeks after she died?"

Blake said thoughtfully, "I shouldn't talk about things like that. Mom and Dad say that I have an overactive imagination. And it makes the other kids think I'm weirder." Uncomfortable, he changed the subject: "Hey! Are you packed? If not, better get going. Mom will be mad if you're not ready when she gets home."

First thing in the morning, the boys would be off to spend time with Uncle Jack, their mother's older brother. He lived in Stuartville, in northern California, about forty miles east of the coastal city of Eureka. Every year, he had invited the family to visit over spring break. This year, because of complicated schedules—their father's business was installing new computer software and their mother was helping their grandmother Ackers settle into a new, assisted-living situation—the boys were flying north on their own to be met by Uncle Jack at the Eureka-Arcata airport.

The two were looking forward to it. Uncle Jack was cool. He wrote scary stories for kids. He had endless tales to tell, tons of DVDs, and tapes of people giving accounts of frightening things that had happened to them. Their parents thought most of what Uncle Jack did or talked about was pretty interesting, too; but their mom sometimes made her brother shut off a DVD or cut short a story that she deemed "too disturbing for the boys"—ignoring the fact that the boys were loving every gory detail.

And there were so many things in their uncle's house to look at that a lifetime wouldn't be long enough. He had plastic models of the Creature from the Black Lagoon and Dracula, a wired-together human skeleton, Ouija boards and tarot decks, blueprints for the starships *Enterprise* and *Galactica*, and bookshelves filled with ghost stories, fictional and true. The library was Blake's favorite thing.

With all this available and only their uncle to decide what was appropriate to read, watch, or hear, the ten days promised thrilling, chilling *bliss*.

Their flight from Los Angeles to Eureka was exciting on its own. Blake felt very grown-up and responsible shepherding Jamie through the San Francisco airport, where they changed from a full-size jet to the sixteen-seater prop plane that took them through the second half of their journey.

Uncle Jack was waiting in the tiny, redwood-sided Eureka-Arcata terminal. Big and bearded and jolly-looking, he wore the patched red-flannel lumberjack shirt and an SF Giants baseball cap that the boys called his "uniform."

He gave Jamie a bear-hug, but shook Blake's hand with

his big paw—a quiet acknowledgment that Blake was fast approaching adulthood. Their uncle was always tuned in to things that most adults would never pick up on.

He joked and chattered almost the whole time they drove to Stuartville through forests of pine and redwood. There was a lot of dampness in the air and a heavy cloud cover. But there were plenty of patches of warm sunlight, too.

Their uncle's good mood slipped only once: when they turned off the main road onto Ridge Road, which ended at the turnaround in front of his house. They passed a big, green, two-story wooden house belonging to the Allard family. It was on a corner lot, set back behind split-rail fences and an expanse of lawn. A double garage stood to one side, with a gravel road connecting to the main road. On the other side was a large doghouse, also painted green, with green shingles on the roof and red trim around the door.

Always in the past, Marco, the Allards' Doberman, would galumph from his doghouse to bark a greeting at the Jeep from just inside the fence. Today, no excited Marco appeared. To Blake, the house looked deserted. Drapes or blinds covered the windows. The garage doors were shut. None of the family's three autos was parked haphazardly along the gravel drive.

"Are the Allards away?" asked Blake.

Their uncle gave him a strange look. "Didn't your parents tell you? The Allards were killed last year. I put it all in one of my long e-mails to your mom."

Blake was shocked. "She never said anything to us." Neither he nor Jamie could pull their eyes away from what was now a place of sadness.

Uncle Jack sighed. "Sometimes I think my sister doesn't read my messages very closely—or at all. I know I'm long-winded and probably put everything including the kitchen sink into my communiqués. Now that I think about it, I'm surprised it didn't come up when we talked."

"Mom's been so busy, with Gran being sick all these months," Blake temporized, eyes still on the house that was—mercifully—soon hidden by a stand of pines. "She's spent more time at Gran's house than she's spent with us. And Gran kept arguing about not wanting someone 'underfoot' all the time and never going to—what do they call it?"

"Assisted living," Uncle Jack said. "I guess I should have been there for both of them, instead of up here with the dogs."

Now Blake was getting uncomfortable, feeling he'd accidentally guilt-tripped his uncle. He was grateful when Jamie piped up, "But how were the Allards killed? Did they crash their car?"

"Some people broke into the house while the Allards were in town. The family unfortunately came back too early. . . ."

"That's awful!" cried Blake. "What about Marco?"

"They killed him first. The police figure he was trying to defend the house."

"Did they catch the guys who did it?" Jamie wondered.

"Not so far. But the police are pretty sure they're somewhere nearby. There's been no more trouble in the immediate area; but there have been one or two break-ins over toward Moss Creek and Ferndale. Luckily, no one else has been hurt."

"Those towns are miles away," said Blake.

"The police think, because of what happened to the Allards, whoever did it won't pull anything back this way again. But I'm still not taking any chances with you guys. While you're here, you keep close to the house. Since I'm here all the time, I keep a pretty sharp eye on things. But you tell me right away if you see anything—*anything*—suspicious."

The three rode the rest of the way to Uncle Jack's place in silence. Their mood improved when his two golden retrievers and Australian shepherd—Alphonse, Gaston, and Sheila—piled out of the screen door to jump all over the boys and their master, vying for attention and trying to nuzzle each other out of the way to get the lion's share of petting. Blake was saddened to recall how Marco had rough-housed with the other dogs when the Allards would stop by the house on their evening walk. *Poor Allards*, thought Blake. *Poor Marco*. Still, it was hard to stay blue with the dogs licking their faces and making them laugh.

Finally Jack shooed the dogs off while they brought in the luggage.

The living room, with its massive fieldstone fireplace, was just as Blake remembered it; the big, polished coffee table—a sliced redwood burl with ragged edges—was covered with magazines like *UFO Today*, *Cemetery Dance*, and *Weird Tales*. Blake could hardly wait to start exploring his uncle's library to see what new treasures awaited.

Because their parents weren't along, Blake got the big second-floor corner room to himself, with its window looking west and south. From the south-facing window he could see over the trees that clustered along Ridge Road to the green-shingled roof of the Allards' house. When he opened the window to let in a little breeze, he imagined for a moment that he could hear a dog barking. Since his uncle's three hounds had been left inside, he knew it wasn't one of them. But there were so many dogs in the area, it could belong to anyone. Still, there was something in the barely heard sound that made Blake think of Marco.

Doghouse

Blake quickly unpacked, then went into the room next door with the bunk beds he usually shared with Jamie. His brother was lying on the top bunk normally assigned to Blake as the oldest. His clothes were strewn across the lower bunk, which was as far as he'd gotten with unpacking. Jamie was playing a game on his Nintendo DS Lite hand-held.

"Aren't you going to finish unpacking?" asked Blake.

"There's plenty of time," Jamie said offhandedly. "Anyway, I can find stuff easier on the bed than in a drawer."

"It's sad about the Allards," said Blake, pushing aside some clothes to sit on the lower bunk.

"Yeah," agreed Jamie. Then a thought struck him. He leaned over the edge of the upper bunk so he could see his brother. "Uncle Jack said whoever did it is probably still hanging around, robbing more people."

"Uh-huh," said Blake, unable to guess where Jamie was headed.

"Maybe you—*we*—could help nail the crooks."

"How?" Blake was completely lost now.

"Use your esp—I mean, ESP—power. You said people who have it sometimes help police solve cases."

Blake snorted. "Get real! Those people are psychics—pros. Besides, do you think the police are going to listen to a kid?"

"Oh," said Jamie, disappointed. He went back to his handheld.

But Blake was thinking, *I wish I* could *help catch whoever killed the Allards and their dog.*

After a late dinner—tamale pie and chocolate sundaes—the three watched *Alien: Resurrection*, one of Uncle Jack's favorites. Though it was nearly midnight before they headed to bed, Blake had trouble getting to sleep. When he did finally drift off, his sleep was troubled by strange dreams. In one, he was in the woods, looking for a path. No moon or stars were visible, but there was a sliver-white sky glow that illuminated everything. He had no idea how he had come here. All he knew was he had to find a path out of the woods or something bad would happen. Now he could hear men's voices behind him. He couldn't understand what they were saying, but he sensed they were looking for him, they were angry, and they were getting closer.

Suddenly, between two silvery tree trunks, a familiar black shape appeared. "Marco!" he called. The dog looked at him, gave a single bark, then turned and ran a little ways into the woods. When Blake didn't follow, the dog looked back over his shoulder and whined, somehow suggesting puzzlement. "I'm coming," Blake called. Marco sprinted into the woods, leading Blake along a path that zigzagged through the trees.

There were angry shouts behind him. His pursuers had found his escape route. The boy ran as fast as he could, but the others soon gained on him.

He broke free of the trees. Before him was an upsweep of silvered lawn. In the far distance, at the crest of this high, steep slope, was the Allard house—no bigger than a dollhouse. Halfway there was Marco's doghouse, looking three times as big as in waking life. The structure was made of shiny metal; the band outlining the door was so bright it seemed painted in quicksilver.

Marco was pacing frantically in front of it. Occasionally he barked at Blake, as if to hurry him along. But the slope kept growing steeper. When the boy risked a look back, he saw three blurry figures had followed him onto the hillside and were getting closer.

The Allard house remained distant and tiny. Blake was sure his only hope was in reaching Marco's house, where the dog was now barking out a stream of ever-more-insistent yelps. But Blake was finding that advancing uphill was like moving through glue.

Voices that now sounded more like growls and snarls—barely human—were almost on top of him.

Somehow he found the ability to slog more quickly toward the doghouse. Marco disappeared inside it a moment before Blake reached it. "Marco!" he called, but there was no answering bark from the pitch-black interior.

A big hand grabbed his right shoulder; a second locked on his left arm, just above the elbow. He twisted to one side, then the other, and broke free for a moment. He had only an instant to choose whether to hurl himself into the darkness of the doghouse or continue struggling uphill, hoping to stay a step ahead of the others.

The blackness in front of him was frightening, but what was behind him was worse.

He plunged through the doorway.

Time seemed to stand still. Then something terrible came roaring out of the dark; at first he thought it was Marco—but it was something else, too. He had only a momentary impression of fiery eyes and hideous jaws in a muzzle twisted by rage. Unable to look, Blake buried his face in his hands. Behind him, the menacing sounds of his pursuers turned to shouts, then screams. But Blake was so overwhelmed by the shock of it all, he was screaming, too.

He was still screaming when he was shaken awake by his uncle. He could see Jamie staring wide-eyed from the doorway. The bedroom was filled with soft, early-morning light.

Doghouse

"Easy, easy," Uncle Jack soothed him, patting Blake's shoulder. "You were having one heckuva nightmare, buddy."

"Guess so," Blake agreed. His voice was raspy from screaming.

"Too many aliens or too much tamale pie," chuckled Uncle Jack. He thought a moment. "Remember anything about it?"

"No," said Blake, happy the dream had fled as he woke up.

"Too bad." His uncle laughed. "I could have worked it into one of my books." He squeezed Blake's shoulder to let his nephew know he was teasing.

Though the details of the dream were gone, the awfulness of it lingered in Blake's mind.

Later that morning, their uncle announced he was heading into town to do some shopping. Jamie chose to go along, but Blake, who was still feeling a little off-kilter, asked to stay. His uncle didn't object: another signal that he respected Blake's new maturity. "But stay close to the house," he warned. "If you see anything or any*one* that looks funny, dial 9-1-1, then call me on my cell. The number's on the desk. There's been too much bad business hereabouts. Promise me—"

"I promise—and I've already memorized your number."

He recited it, and Uncle Jack nodded. "Aces! Okay, we're off."

After they left, Blake read for a while, but he quickly grew restless and abandoned his book. He would have played with the dogs, but they'd gone into town, too. They loved to ride in the Jeep, their heads hanging out the open windows, tongues lolling, soaking up the sun and the wind and the smells.

This made Blake think of Marco, standing foursquare in the flatbed of the Allards' pickup. *He loved life, too, poor pup. They all died. It's so unfair.*

He shoved his hands in his jeans pockets and began walking with no particular goal in mind. Soon he found himself on the path that led through the trees to the Allards' place. He knew he was stretching the bounds of his uncle's "stay close to the house" rule—but the adjoining property wasn't *that* far, he reasoned.

The wooded stretch was lovely, and it lifted his spirits. But when he stepped out on the Allards' land, he felt some of his early-morning, post-nightmare anxiety and gloom descend. The area looked so lonely: the house with curtains and shades pulled, the closed garage and empty gravel drive, and, saddest of all, the doghouse, with the dented tin water dish beside it, bearing, in fading letters, the name MARCO.

Doghouse

The weather changed abruptly. The sun vanished; Blake saw thickening drifts of high fog flowing in from the Pacific Ocean far to the west. There was a sudden chill in the air as the mild breeze grew into a steady draft. Birds and crickets pretty much ceased their songs.

With a glance at the doghouse, he climbed onto the Allards' porch. Piles of dried leaves and bunches of pine and redwood needles crunched underfoot. He tried the front doorknob, but the place was locked up tight.

Remembering something that he'd read in one of Uncle Jack's books, he pressed his hands against the glass panes of the doors, fingers splayed out, closed his eyes, and imagined that he could receive messages from beyond. But, if there was some psychic energy around, he couldn't tune in to it.

It seemed to him that the house wasn't haunted—except to the degree that it brought back memories of the former owners.

He wandered over to poor old Marco's doghouse. Gently, he touched the roof.

Blake snatched back his fingers. He'd felt something like an electric shock. At the same moment, he'd had a vision of Marco rushing toward him across a vast, dark expanse: only it *wasn't* just Marco. It was like two creatures occupying the same body. One was the loving dog he knew well; the other was a beast with red eyes and slavering jaws that seemed to have ripped free of Blake's nightmare, which he suddenly recalled in way-too-vivid detail.

Then something shifted. He wasn't looking at dogs from heaven or hell or wherever: He clearly saw three men at the edge of the woods, staring up at the Allard house, where a porch light shone that hadn't been on a moment before. The day was dark, as though several hours had passed.

The watchers were not the shadowy, faceless, almost shapeless figures of his dreams. They were three all-too-human monsters who were planning to "get rid of the dog—and anyone else who crosses us." He saw and heard them clearly: one guy, short but muscular, looking like someone who worked out in a gym, holding a gun; one, half a head taller but flabby-looking; and the third, youngest-looking of all. Something made Blake think the taller man might be the brother of this last guy, whose head swiveled side to side as he asked, "Are we being watched? I got this creepy feeling."

"Knock it off," said Body Builder, clearly the leader. "The family's gone, and there's no one around." They headed toward the doghouse. Marco appeared, growling, sensing something amiss. The leader raised his gun—

Then the vision was gone. But Blake was sure he'd seen the criminals who had killed the Allards and Marco.

Doghouse

Blake stood for a moment, shaking. A quick survey of his surroundings revealed no ghost dogs or criminals. It was midafternoon again. No light burned on the porch.

Still feeling light-headed, he started back to Uncle Jack's.

The others weren't home yet, so taking some Oreos and chocolate milk into the library, he rooted through his uncle's collection for books on animal ghosts. He was surprised to find there were quite a number of them.

He learned some interesting things: Stories of ghost dogs were common all around the world. They sometimes appeared as big white or black creatures with glowing or fiery eyes and tongues. Occasionally, one was *headless*. He read about someone robbing a haunted house who was chased away by two ghost dogs. Blake also found the story of a ghostly dog that returned to help clear his master who was charged with murder. But a ghostly black dog could mean trouble. To be haunted by one meant misery or bad luck. In England, such creatures were thought to linger where a murder or some other crime had been committed.

Closing the last book, Blake wondered if he had encountered Marco's ghost earlier in the day. Maybe what he'd envisioned had been a bit of the dog's memory of that awful crime. Did that mean the animal's spirit was still around? Why? Anger seemed the best guess. Remembering the snarling demon dog that replaced easygoing Marco, he shuddered. It seemed the animal's rage was directed at the men who had committed the crime. But there was something so raw and mindless in that recollected emotion that he wondered if such a ghostly creature would be a danger to anyone whose path he crossed, not just the guilty.

He heard the squeal of brakes; a moment later, the Jeep doors slammed. He took his dirty dishes into the kitchen and went to help unload the groceries.

At dinner, Blake asked, "Uncle Jack, do you believe in ghosts? I know you're always writing about them. But do you *really* think there are such things?"

The man considered. "I've never actually seen one. But I believe it's quite possible. I guess I'm like that guy who said, 'I don't believe in ghosts, but I'm afraid of them.' I find them interesting to read about, fun to write about, but I don't think I ever want to meet one up close."

"What about animal ghosts?"

"Lots of people believe they exist. If people have spirits, why not at least the more-evolved animals like monkeys, cats, or dogs?"

"I thought I saw the ghost of Marco. But he was angry.

He scared me." Blake carefully avoided saying *where* he had had his ghostly encounter.

"He'd have every right to be," Jack responded. "Cut off by greed and cruelty from life and from the humans he deeply loved." He shook his head.

"I think I saw the guys who did it."

"What? Where?"

"In a kind of dream, only I was awake. Maybe it was a vision. I don't know. I think I should tell the police."

"Not a good idea. I know Sheriff Madigan. He's the last person who'd believe that you got some kind of psychic message. And he'd probably be annoyed and say you were interfering. No"—he shook his head firmly—"I don't want you mixed up in this ugliness. Let the police handle it. Look, I don't set many rules, but this is one you'd better make up your mind to follow: Stay nearby and stay out of trouble. Agreed?"

Blake nodded.

Uncle Jack turned to Jamie. "The same applies to you."

"I don't even like ghosts," Jamie said.

"Okay, let's do the dishes and have a hand of draw poker—penny limit."

Blake and Jamie were careful to keep away from the Allard place for the next couple of days. While their uncle worked at the computer in his office, they hiked to the top of nearby Fairview Hill, waded in the creek on the eastern edge of the property, and generally goofed off.

On Friday, their uncle suggested, "Let's take in the monster double-header at the cinema. It's two of my favorites, *Creature from the Black Lagoon* and *It Came from Outer Space*—both in 3-D, with genuine cellophane-and-cardboard 3-D glasses."

After three burgers washed down with double-choc malts at the drive-in, Uncle Jack stopped at the gas station on the way to Stuartville's small movie house.

While his uncle was pumping gas and Jamie was buying candy in the mini mart, Blake sat in the Jeep, absently staring out his rolled-down window.

A grimy black Ford SUV pulled into the area on the other side of the row of gas pumps. Two guys climbed out. One swiped his credit card and began filling the tank; Blake recognized Body Builder right away. Flab used a squeegee to wash the windshield. A third, younger than the others, climbed out of the backseat and went into the mini mart. Punk, Blake nicknamed him.

A shudder ran through Blake like iced electricity. He was vaguely aware that his uncle had finished filling their own vehicle and had gone to find Jamie. He kept his eyes on the two older men. Suddenly someone demanded, "What're you lookin' at, weirdo?"

Blake spun around and came face-to-face with the crew-cut Punk.

"Noth—" Blake said, too startled to get the whole word out.

"Me and my buddies don't like being stared at—especially by weirdos."

"I wasn't—" Blake said, retreating deeper into the car. He could see the guy's friends watching from the other side of the pumping station island.

"Problem?" asked Uncle Jack, returning with Jamie in tow.

"Nah," said the young guy, moving away toward the SUV.

"Well, move along. Jamie, into the car. I don't want to miss the opening credits of *Creature*." Blake, staring straight ahead, was aware of three sets of eyes watching him and the Jeep as they pulled out of the station.

"What was that all about?" Uncle John asked.

"They're the guys I saw in my vision," the boy answered, finally turning to look back. The SUV was gone. "The ones who did what they did to the Allards."

"I could believe it: They're bad news. But no one's going to believe your vision, Blake. Stay out of this, and here's rule number two: Don't talk to—don't even look cross-eyed at—those guys if you ever spot them again. Promise."

"Yeah," Blake agreed.

"And, Jamie—"

"I know, that goes for me, too," Jamie said, sounding bored. "I don't care."

Jamie and Uncle Jack loved the double feature, but Blake couldn't get the encounter at the gas station out of his mind. And he was haunted later by dreams of blazing eyes and slavering fangs and screams, so he awoke as tired as if he hadn't slept at all.

The next morning, after much inner debate, Blake decided to take action. Closing his bedroom door, he pulled his cell phone from the bottom of his overnight case. He'd found the sheriff's number in the phone book. Since his dad had insisted that the family cells have blocked numbers, he felt he could make his call safely, anonymously.

His hand shook as he punched in the number. A woman's voice assured him that he had reached the sheriff's office and asked how she could direct his call.

"I want to talk to the sheriff," he said, trying to deepen his voice.

"Is this an emergency?"

"Not exactly. Kinda. Could I just talk to the sheriff?"

"What is this in regard to?"

"The Allard killings. Them and their dog," Blake blurted out.

"Please hold the line."

A moment later, an impatient male voice cut in. "Who is this, and what do you know?"

"I can't give you my name."

A waiting silence.

"I know who did it—killed the Allards and their dog."

Another silence. Waiting.

"Three guys." He described them from his vision and from the gas station.

"Their names?"

"I don't know. But they hang around town a lot."

"And you know they committed this crime how?"

"I'm a psychic. I have ESP. I've helped other police departments solve crimes before," he said, rushing through the story he'd prepared.

"Uh-huh. And what law enforcement agencies were those?"

"I signed papers that say I can't tell," he said. He'd remembered something like that from a movie he'd seen.

There was a long sigh on the other end of the phone. To Blake, it sounded somewhere between tired and angry.

Then the sheriff said, "Young man, you are wasting my time and the taxpayers' money. I don't know what your beef is with the guys you were describing—and I know who they are, whether you give me their names or not—but we've checked them out. They were nowhere near the scene of the crime. We've got half a dozen witnesses say they were in Eureka that night."

"They're lying—" Blake protested.

"Only one liar," said the sheriff, "and it isn't the witnesses."

The phone went dead.

Well, Blake thought. *Didn't Uncle Jack warn me?*

He didn't know what to do next. *Maybe there's nothing to do*, he concluded. They were within a few days of returning home, their visit nearly over. He made up his mind: *Let it go*.

But the issue wouldn't let go of him. His dreams were plagued with images of Marco, morphing from friendly to ferocious, and three figures chasing him across a nightmare version of the Allards' property.

Then, on the Friday before he and Jamie were to fly home, they spent the afternoon with Uncle Jack. He'd finished the first draft of his new book and needed downtime before he began revising it.

So they had a picnic in the park at the edge of town.

Doghouse

While his uncle and brother tossed a baseball, Blake headed through the trees toward the duck pond. He'd collected some scraps from lunch to feed them.

But when he was almost there, a fistful of his shirt was suddenly grabbed by a meaty hand. He was jerked around to see Body Builder. Flabby and Punk weren't far away, leaning against the trunk of an oak.

"Just wanted to say hi. We've been looking for you," Body Builder said as Blake tried to squirm free. "Seems some kid was trying to make trouble for us with the sheriff."

"I didn't—I don't . . ." Blake began.

"I don't believe in coincidence," said the guy. "You checking us out one night and the sheriff getting an anonymous call from a kid the next day is just too big a coincidence for me to buy." He hauled Blake so close the boy nearly gagged on his onion-and-garlic breath; he was aware of the other two drawing close to flank their leader.

"My uncle—"

His captor shook him like a rag doll. "Quiet! What we want to know is: What do you *think* you know, little man?"

"You did it!" Blake screamed. He twisted violently and felt several buttons pop off his shirt. Then cloth ripped, and he was running away, leaving a piece of his shirt in the man's fist.

Blake ran blindly back toward the picnic area. He

expected to hear the sounds of pursuit, but all he heard was Body Builder's taunt, "You can run, but you can't hide. You're toast, little man."

"What happened to you?" his uncle asked, when he stopped to catch his breath after charging across the meadow to where Uncle Jack and Jamie were still playing catch.

"Those . . . those guys. From the gas station. After me." He waved vaguely toward the clump of trees.

His uncle shaded his eyes and took a long look. "There's no one there."

"They were. They've been looking for me: One said so. He tore my shirt."

"Why are they on your case?"

"Just because I was staring at them. Maybe they think I know something."

"I'm going to call the sheriff as soon as we get home," Uncle Jack said.

Blake was relieved. He'd figured his uncle would insist on going to the sheriff's office in person, where the sheriff would have recognized his voice as the troublemaking kid who claimed to be a psychic. Then his uncle would find out about his broken promise.

All the way back to Ridge Road, he stayed in the

backseat, watching to see if they were being followed. Once or twice he thought he saw the black SUV behind them, but he couldn't be sure.

When their uncle finished talking to the sheriff, all he said was "They're going to keep an eye on things."

That Saturday, Blake sat on the porch reading a laugh-out-loud fantasy novel by Terry Pratchett, one of his uncle's favorite authors, whom Blake had become addicted to. His uncle was upstairs composing one of his "long-winded" e-mails to a writer friend. Jamie had wanted to make one last hike to visit the creek, and his uncle had given permission. Suddenly, there was a squeal of brakes, a sickening thump, and the howling of an animal in pain. Startled, Blake shot to his feet, the copy of *The Color of Magic* slipping to the floor. He shaded his eyes against the noonday glare and saw a gray pickup stopped in the road just below. A man climbed out and knelt beside a golden brown heap beside the left front tire. A woman, wringing her hands, was alternately looking down at what was on the ground and looking all around, as if for help.

In an instant, Blake realized what had happened. One of his uncle's retrievers, Alphonse, had been hit. Now he could see the other two dogs nervously circling just beyond the two people.

Uncle Jack hurtled through the front door a moment later. "What—" he began.

"They hit Alphonse," Blake shouted over his shoulder. He was running toward the road, with his uncle right behind.

The retriever was in great pain, but clearly very much alive.

"They just ran out in front of me," the man explained. But Uncle Jack was too concerned with the dog to pay attention.

The woman had started to cry. Blake wanted to help but couldn't think how. "We've got to get him to the vet, fast!" said Uncle Jack.

"Put him in the back of the truck. You can stay with him. The pet emergency hospital is just down the road."

Gently, Uncle Jack, with the other man's help, put Alphonse, shuddering and whining and very frightened, in the bed of the truck. Then Uncle Jack climbed in. He yelled to Blake, "Put the other dogs in the house. Then go check on Jamie. Be sure he's all right. I want both of you back at the house pronto."

The man and the woman got into the cab of the truck, slammed the doors shut, and the pickup roared down the road.

When the vehicle raced around a bend in the road,

Doghouse

Blake, still in shock from the accident, called to Gaston and Sheila. The two dogs followed him into the house. Once they were settled, he set off for the creek to find his brother.

The woods were so peaceful compared to the scene he'd just witnessed that he decided it wouldn't hurt to take a few minutes and calm down.

When he told Jamie what had happened, the younger boy said, "I hope Alphonse doesn't die. That would be awful after what happened to Marco." They were sitting on a fallen log, tossing stones into the water. Suddenly, Jamie asked, "Do you think they'll ever get those guys for what they did to the Allards?"

"I hope so," Blake said, sending a stone skipping across the water with such force that it buried itself in some ferns on the other side of the stream.

"What about Marco? Do you think he'll always have to stay there, hanging out, waiting for the Allards?" Jamie fully believed Blake had seen the ghost dog.

His brother shrugged. "Beats me. Maybe he'll realize they're not coming back and go wherever dog ghosts go. Or maybe he'll just stay around, getting angrier and meaner and stronger, until he can really hurt someone."

"But Marco was so friendly."

"Not the one in my dreams. I mean, some of the times

he seemed like the dog we knew—but then he'd change into something scary, like a monster." Blake shuddered. He skimmed one last rock and then said, "We'd better start back."

They were so busy talking when they left the woods they didn't register anything wrong until three figures rose up from lounge chairs on the redwood deck at the back of their uncle's house.

"It's them," said Blake. He put his hand reassuringly on his brother's shoulder.

Body Builder, Flab, and Punk came to the edge of the deck, pausing where broad steps dropped down to the gravel path that led to the two boys.

"Where's Uncle Jack?" Jamie asked in a frightened whisper.

"Not back yet, I guess." Blake never took his eyes off the men, who remained in place.

Then Body Builder said, "Come on up, guys. We need to powwow a little."

Keeping his voice very low, Blake told his brother, "When I count to three, you run for the creek and try to hide. I'm going to run to the Allard place. I don't think they'll follow you. It's me they're worried about."

Jamie started to protest, but Blake said, "*Just do it*. One, two . . ."

Doghouse

Now the men were descending the steps, slowly, their eyes locked on the frightened boys.

"THREE!" shouted Blake. He saw Jamie break for the shelter of the woods they had just left, while he bolted for the narrow path to the Allard place. Once there, he hoped to flag down a car and get some help.

He had guessed right: The men ignored Jamie and came pounding after him. He followed the twisty path at breakneck speed—thankful that he'd traveled it often enough to know its turns and bends and where low-hanging tree branches waited to ambush the unwary. He could hear his pursuers crashing along behind him, alternately shouting encouragement to each other and warning him what they were going to do when they caught him. The threats made him run faster than ever.

The shadows under the trees were deepening as the afternoon waned. Blake felt a little safer in the gathering dusk. There was another bellow behind him and a lot of cursing. He guessed someone had run into a low branch or caught a foot in one of the leaf-filled holes that lay like mini pitfalls for the careless. He began to think he might make it to safety, after all. A few moments later, he flung himself out of the trees and onto the sweep of lawn that led to the house and the doghouse.

As he charged up the hill to circle the house and head

for the road beyond, he was reminded of his first nightmare. It was too much like this moment. A second later, the two older men burst from the tree line, while Punk came limping behind.

Blake thought he had enough lead, but a rock whizzed by his head an instant later. He guessed they weren't shooting to avoid attracting attention. A second stone hit him squarely between the shoulder blades. The impact knocked the wind out of him and sent him tumbling onto the grass. He was gasping for breath, sprawled full-length so near Marco's doghouse that one outflung hand rested beside the door.

Too stunned to do more than fight for breath, Blake heard the three men approaching. They were laughing, and Body Builder was saying to the others, "Good thing I haven't lost my pitching arm, right?"

Then they hauled Blake into a sitting position. He was still having trouble breathing. "Lean him against the doghouse," said Body Builder. He and Flab propped the boy against the side. Punk was sitting cross-legged on the grass, rubbing a sore ankle.

The older men hunkered down on either side of Blake, sitting on their heels. Body Builder slapped the boy lightly, asking, "Coming around, little man?"

Blake weakly tried to bat the other's hand aside, but the

guy ignored him and slapped harder. "Time to tell me a few things before I really lose my temper." He gave another slap for emphasis.

Then Punk began to shriek. The others could see around the corner of the doghouse to where the youngest hood was scrambling backward on his hands and haunches with a look of horror fixed on the doghouse entrance.

There was a sudden explosion of darkness from the interior. It was a giant black dog, moving with incredible swiftness. His eyes were on fire; a fringe of flame danced across his muzzle. The monster clamped its jaws on Punk's neck. The unfortunate burst into flame. A moment later, there was just a pile of ash being churned by the evening breeze.

Body Builder and Flab didn't hesitate. They took off running toward the road, but the dog was on Flab in two bounds. Screaming, the man flamed out of existence. For an instant, it looked like Body Builder might get away. Then the dog slammed into him, gripping his back. Terrified, Blake watched as the man's skin turned to what looked like charred leather. Body Builder shriveled to half his size before he burst into flames like his buddies.

Blake tried to run away, but he was still so stunned by everything, he could only struggle to his feet, using the doghouse for support.

Doghouse

The monster hound turned its fiery eyes on him. It began loping toward him with an evil, almost human grin, as if it knew the boy couldn't escape. Blake wondered again if the creature was so filled with blazing hatred that any living person was an enemy.

The quaking boy could feel the heat radiating from the dog. Under the immense pads of its feet, the grass crisped and burned, leaving puffs of smoke behind.

Blake edged to the corner of the doghouse, took a shaky step away, and realized that, without the support, his legs were not going to hold him up. Like a broken doll, he collapsed on the lawn.

The devil from his dreams was almost upon him. Uselessly, he held up one hand, palm out, feeling the skin start to heat even as he said, "No, Marco. Good Marco. It's me, Blake."

Unexpectedly, the dog stood still, cocked its head to one side, as if puzzled, and regarded Blake closely. After a moment the creature gave a curious whine. Then, to Blake's astonishment, it began to change, the fearsome bulk dwindling to the shape and size of Marco as he had been in life. The fire left his eyes; they became the gentle, liquid brown eyes of the old Marco.

When the transformation was complete, Blake stretched out a tentative hand toward the ghost dog. Marco came to him. The boy reached down and imagined he was petting him as he had always done, even though his hand moved through empty air. But the dog seemed to sense something. There was no fire now, only a soft coolness that soothed his burned palm.

Then Marco's ears pricked up, as though he'd heard one of those dog whistles too high-pitched for human ears. A minute later, Marco was charging up the hill toward the house. But the closer he got, the fainter his shape became. Long before he reached the front porch steps, he had vanished completely.

"Good luck, boy," Blake whispered. "I hope you find them waiting for you."

The evening breeze stirred bits of charred grass and caught ashes in eddies, then scattered them. *No one would believe me,* Blake thought, then added ruefully, *I don't believe it myself.*

By the time he met his frantically searching uncle, he could give only a confused account of managing to run away and elude his pursuers. He knew there would be many more questions. But the real story would always be—had to be—untold.

The Haunted Mansion

Early one morning in summer, Eric Webster was strolling the shore on Findings Island, one of North Carolina's wonderful warm-water beaches, so different from the cold, pounding surf of his and his father's northern California home. These barrier islands protect the Carolina coast. To reach Findings, he and his father had driven south along State Highway 12, which linked the islands, a ferry filling in where the road failed at Hatteras Inlet. They'd passed Kitty Hawk (the base from which the Wright Brothers flew the first heavier-than-air machine), Nags Head (pirates had prowled the waters), then scenic Ocracoke and Portsmouth islands—all part of the Outer Banks.

Eric was in North Carolina so his father, Brad, who

had grown up in the area, could go surf fishing. They were staying at the Comer's and Goer's Inn, "comers and goers" being the local name for tourists. (The locals called themselves "bankers.") The place overlooked Winnard Beach, a long, lonely stretch of sand facing the Atlantic. On the other side of the lean island was Lee'urd Beach, fronting the gentler, warmer waters of thirty-mile-wide Pamlico Sound, beyond which lay the Carolina mainland. Inland was a swamp forest of virgin cypress called Tsikilili Pond and Creek.

The inn, two stories of weathered wood, was owned and operated by Denice—Neesy—Cinders and her sister, Aunt Rilla. Neesy's son, Tyler, who was Eric's age (ten), helped out at the inn a lot. The food alone made it a paradise in Eric's mind: Spaghetti New Orleans, with lots of fresh shrimp; chicken pie; layered potato salad; pumpkin muffins; shortcake biscuits with sweetened berries and lemon ice cream. These were just some of the goodies that found their way to the dining table.

Eric and Tyler had bonded instantly and spent as much time as they could together. Tyler's mother was black, but his father (who had died some years before) was a full-blood Cherokee; Tyler felt equally proud of both bloodlines. And the boy had an inexhaustible supply of tales from his ancestral traditions. Tyler was a storehouse of island lore. He swore his cousin Hattie had seen a fearsome whangdoodle. "That thing has big balls of green fire for eyes. It's long as a goat, high as a cow, and has ears like a mule. It's all gray and woolly, and it goes, '*Ye-e-e-ow-ow-ow!*'" Tyler screamed the last into Eric's ear, making him jump. Then the two laughed like a pair of lunatics.

Tyler knew about the Cherokee woman monster Utlunta, who killed people with a sharp, stony forefinger on her right hand. "You come too close," Tyler said, "and, man, she'll stab you and rip out your liver and eat it."

"That's so gross," said Eric, making a face.

There were endless accounts by Tyler of beings like the Gray Man of Hatteras, who roams the shores and warns people to find safe ground when a storm is coming. The Sea Hag of Portsmouth was a powerful witch who didn't ride a broom. Instead she rode the long steering oar of a whaling ship she had caused to sink, using the oar blade like a rudder when she flew through the air.

But best, as far as Eric was concerned, were the stories of pirates who prowled the outer banks: "Calico Jack" Rackham, Blackbeard, Anne Bonny, and Mad Daniel Durand, who plagued the Caribbean and Outer Banks, and was rumored to have hidden his treasure on Findings and several nearby islands.

One afternoon, the boys sat side by side on a driftwood

log. Eric was staring out over the wave-capped water, under a nearly cloudless expanse of blue skies; Tyler was sketching in the sand with the end of a sharp stick. They munched hot peppered pecans Tyler had brought along in a little paper sack.

Suddenly Tyler tossed the stick away, sending it spinning to scatter a flock of gulls who rose protesting into the air.

"We're friends, right?" he asked Eric.

"Sure," Eric insisted.

"Good enough friends so that I can trust you with a secret?"

"I can keep a secret."

"You remember those stories I told about that pirate, Mad Daniel Durand?"

"Sure. Didn't you say he used Findings Island here as his home base? At least, that's the story you told me."

"It's more than a story. I got proof."

"What kind of proof?"

"A house, over to Lee'urd Beach, where Durand used to visit his girlfriend who lived there."

Suspicious, Eric asked, "How come I haven't heard of the place before?"

"Bankers keep it secret. It's haunted, folks say. And too

much messin' with the ghosts will bring bad luck—maybe a storm, maybe worse."

"Prove it," Eric challenged.

"I'll show you, but you got to be cool."

"I can be cool," replied Eric, skepticism and excitement filling him equally. "Let's go."

Tyler stuffed what was left of the spiced pecans into his pocket. Then he led them by a torturous path along the creek and around the south end of Tsikilili Pond. They had to go carefully. There were sinkholes; twice Eric saw snakes that Tyler warned were poisonous; clouds of gnats plagued them.

"I see why most people stay away from here," Eric grumbled.

"Wanna turn back?"

"No way."

They trudged along, and by the time they reached the decaying house that was rumored to be haunted, Tyler had filled Eric in on the most important details.

The place had been built back in colonial times by a rich merchant named Ezra Summerton. The man had made his fortune on the mainland in Beaufort, but he decided to retire to Findings Island for reasons of his own. He was a widower, with one daughter, Emily. According to Tyler, the massive brick mansion was said to be haunted by the ghost of Emily Summerton, who had lived in the house with her aged father and stayed on with a few servants after the old man's death. The shuttered windows of the house, which was smothered in vines and brush, brooded over the remains of what must have once been a fancy garden. Beyond the house, the boys could clearly see the rippling blue waters of Pamlico Sound.

While they stood looking at the scene, Tyler commented, "For a couple of hundred years, folks hereabouts have said they see a ghost ship sailing out there." He waved toward the sound. "Most people think it's the long-lost *Sea Devil*, the ship that belonged to Mad Daniel Durand. Only folks call him Headless Dan now, 'cause he died by having his head cut off. Folks say the ship mostly drifts in circles, because Dan can't see to steer a proper course."

"I hadn't heard *that* part," said Eric eagerly. "How'd it happen?"

"Story is, Mad Dan was in love with Emily Summerton, but her father hated the pirates who were robbing folks and messing with ships and business and stuff. They say that Mad Dan and Emily would meet secretly. Supposedly one of her maids would carry messages back and forth between them. They even say that Emily helped him hide a lot of his treasure in the house, right under her father's nose. She helped Dan to spite the old man, I guess. She and her father didn't get along. The old man could be cruel and tight as all get-out with his money.

"Gal kind of went nuts when she found her father and some other rich folks had hired two ships to go after Dan. She tried to warn him, but her father found out. The message was never delivered. There was a big old battle, and one of Summerton's ships was sunk, but so was the *Sea Devil*. Supposedly Dan, who was badly wounded, escaped in a rowboat to Findings Island. Somehow, he made his way to Summerton's house, looking for Emily, hoping for her help, because he was pretty messed up. He was probably hoping to get back some of his gold, too. But Emily's father spotted him, ambushed the wounded pirate, and cut off his head and then hid it."

Tyler lowered his voice dramatically as he continued. "Ezra had an old slave woman from Africa, who knew some heavy witch-doctor-type magic. She put a spell on the head so that Dan would never be whole again or rest until living hands 'brought what was hidden to light.' At least, that's what I heard. The rest of the story is that the old man sealed up Dan's body in a chest with some of his treasure, but he put the pirate's head in a secret place. No one will ever find it, I guess. The old man died without telling anyone where any gold or the head was hidden.

They say Ezra was found dead in his bed one morning. Had a look on his face made folks think he was scared to death."

Grinning, Tyler said, "You ask me, Mad Dan wasn't the only crazy around. From that time on, you can sometimes hear his ghost howling. That means a storm's coming. He yells because he's still mad about his missing head."

"You said he can't see without his head. How can he yell if he's missing it?" Eric challenged him.

"I don't know," Tyler answered impatiently. "It's just something I heard. How should I know how ghosts go about their business?"

"What happened to Emily?"

Tyler shrugged. "They say she just pined away for Dan. She had herself buried in some kind of 'crystal' ball gown the pirate gave her. Her grave is supposed to be right around here. They say the ghosts of Emily and, sometimes, Dan still wander the house."

The ghosts interested Eric, but he was more intrigued by the part of the story about Headless Dan's hiding a fortune somewhere in the house.

"Hasn't anyone tried to find the treasure?" asked Eric.

"Sure. Plenty of times. Most give up. Some have been scared away by ghosts. Some just disappear: No one knows what happened to 'em. And there's another problem: Old

Rufus. He's a squatter who lives in the house part of the time. At other times he goes off no one knows where. When he's around, he feels he has to protect the place, so he runs people off."

"Is he there now?"

"Dunno."

"Let's take a closer look," Eric suggested.

Tyler hesitated, but came along when Eric teased, "If you're scared, I'll go by myself." But then, Eric whispered, "Don't worry—we'll be careful."

Using commando tactics, the boys, crouching low, ducked and darted from tree to shrub across the overgrown garden at the front of the house. They regrouped behind a big palmetto tree a short distance from the warped and sun-bleached front porch. The shutters upstairs and down were fastened tight, but Tyler nudged his friend and pointed to a lower-floor window at the left corner of the house where one of the matching shutters had nearly fallen off and was tilted to one side. The dark triangle it revealed promised a peek inside. Signaling for his buddy to follow quietly, Eric made a last dash for the porch. He was up the steps and almost to his goal before Tyler followed.

Eric bent to look through the window; an instant later, he felt Tyler's head touching his as they both peered through the gap. There wasn't much to see. In the gloom they could just make out a big, high-ceilinged room, and hulking shapes—furniture, Eric supposed—were scattered around. A few pale shapes startled him, until he realized that some of the furniture was covered with white sheets.

"I don't think there's anyone here," he whispered.

Whatever Tyler started to say in reply was drowned out by a bellow. An old black man with a white beard and fringe of hair, spindly arms and legs jutting out from dirty and patched overalls, yanked open the front door. The screech of rusted hinges added to the drama.

He advanced on the boys, limping but still at a good clip. He was waving a club—it might have been the leg of a small table—over his head. All the time he kept shouting, "You thievin' boys! Come to lift what you can! You snotteries!" Eric couldn't understand half of what he heard, but the anger was unmistakable. "I'll bus' your heads."

The boys weren't about to wait and see if he meant what he threatened. They took off running while the old man lumbered down the short flight of front steps after them, still bellowing and slashing the air with his club. Even when they could no longer hear him, the boys kept running until they reached the edge of Tsikilili Pond. There, Eric slipped in the weedy mud, and Tyler, who had been looking behind for a sign of Rufus, crashed over him. The two wound up slipping and sliding in the swampy ooze. When they were sure the old man wasn't following them, they climbed out, scraped off as much mud and slime as they could, then set out toward the Comer's and Goer's Inn.

"My mom and auntie aren't gonna like this," said Tyler, brushing off some of the residue that was drying into smelly clumps.

"Say we were messing around and had an accident," Eric advised him. "All kids get messy sometimes. Just don't say anything about the house or Rufus."

"Don't worry. I'm *never* supposed to go near that place. Aunt Rilla says it's got bad juju. My mom doesn't believe that, but she's afraid I'd get hurt there."

"Well, yeah," said Eric, "getting your head *bus'* would probably hurt." At this, the two began to laugh, letting go the last of their fear in a burst of giggles. When they'd calmed down, Eric, suddenly serious, said, "I still want to get into that house and look for pirate treasure. Is Rufus *always* there?"

"No. I told you: Sometimes he just goes . . . away. But no one knows when." Suddenly he snapped his fingers. "Friday is the big fish fry in town. If Rufus is around, he never misses the chance to get free food and drinks. He usually passes out on the beach. If it rains, Reverend Leach lets him sleep in the Baptist church basement."

"Yeah," Eric said. "When everyone's asleep, we can meet and check out Summerton House."

"At night?"

"You *are* some kind of a wuss. This is a great chance. We might find that treasure. We'll be rich and famous." Then he lowered his voice and said, "We might see Emily's ghost. Or even Dan without his head." He made ghostly sounds. When Tyler didn't respond, he started making hen clucks. "*Chick-chick-chicken. Chick——*"

"All right, I'll go. Just shut up."

Eric was secretly relieved; he really had been afraid that he wouldn't dare go on the midnight adventure alone, for all his pretended courage.

Fortunately, neither Eric's dad nor Tyler's mom and aunt made too much of the boys' muddy accident. Warnings to clean up and be more careful were as bad as it got.

The fish fry, held in the community hall, was a mix of music and dancing and laughter and tons of good food. Eric gladly pigged out on fried shrimp, flounder, catfish, oysters smothered in Neesy Cinders's homemade tartar sauce and accompanied by coleslaw, french fries, and Aunt Rilla's legendary hush puppies. There was plenty of sweet tea for the locals and unsweetened for most visitors. There were beer and other drinks, but the most popular choice was what Tyler laughingly called "gigglesoup—you know, *moonshine*." As they ate, the boys watched Rufus and stayed out of his way. But Tyler was pretty sure the old man wouldn't recognize them. He pointed out that Rufus was rarely without a mason jar of gigglesoup. "He's gonna sleep till the cows come home tomorrow," Tyler said. "That's fine for us."

Eric was having such fun, he'd half forgotten their plan to sneak out to the deserted Summerton place. Enjoying the good time, he was sorry that he'd pushed Tyler to join him. He thought about canceling, but he didn't want to face the razzing that Tyler would give him if *he* "chickened out."

That night, when he was sure that his father and the rest of the guests and staff at the inn were asleep, Eric mounded his pillows and one blanket on the bed to make it look like he was there. Then, slipping out the door of the room the father and son shared, he made his way slowly to the ground floor, taking care to avoid those spots on the stairway where he'd noticed squeaks earlier in the week.

Tyler was waiting for him just outside the front door. They hurried a short distance from the house and then stopped to be sure they had everything they needed. Tyler had brought a hammer, crowbar, screwdriver, two cans of cola, a big flashlight, and a few other things. Eric had his father's battery-powered lantern, a coil of rope, two Power-Bars, and a canvas bag he hoped to use to carry off jewels and gold doubloons. As they went along, the boys poked fun at each other's fears and pretended they were feeling none of their own.

The moon was high; the night was mild. Eric still found it amazing how many stars he could see when he was away from the city glow of San Jose in California. But as they trekked along, dark clouds began scudding across the sky, forcing the moon and stars to play what Tyler called "all-hid." The wind, though still fairly warm, was rising. In short order, the night sky had grown much darker. They had to use their flashlights to find their path and avoid getting too close to Tsikilili Pond.

Lightning flashed. A lukewarm rain began to fall half-heartedly. Eric was glad to see, when they topped a rise, the bulky shadow of Summerton House ahead of them.

Sure that Rufus was sound asleep in some corner of the church basement, they ran directly to the house. It took only a few minutes, working with Tyler's crowbar, for them to pry the loose shutter back far enough and then jimmy the window beyond so they could climb through, one after the other. On impulse, Eric closed the window when they were inside.

The Haunted Mansion

Around them, the house seemed to stir and mutter as the storm outside grew.

"Where should we start looking for the treasure?" asked Tyler, his voice a whisper, even though there was no one around to hear except Eric. Tyler was using his flashlight. Eric was keeping his lantern to use later.

"The basement," said Eric, who'd been giving the matter a lot of thought. "There must be one. And pirates always buried their treasures. It would make sense for a pirate to stick to his old way of doing things." He glanced at his watch. A few minutes before midnight. They'd have a couple of hours to search before heading back.

But they hadn't taken two steps into the hall in their search for a way into the basement they were certain lay beneath, when there was suddenly a rush of wind past them to the stairway that climbed steeply up into pitch blackness.

That wind couldn't have come from outside, Eric thought. *I closed the window, and nothing else was open.*

Up the stairs it swirled, churning years of dust and debris into a whirlwind that grew and grew until it reached the head of the stairs. There, the churning air began to glow like captured moonlight. Then, slowly, it began to change into the transparent form of a woman.

"That's the ghost of Emily Summerton," Eric said, unable to take his eyes off the figure. He was aware of a terrified Tyler bobbing his head up and down like one of those nodding toys Eric sometimes saw in the back window of a car. The flashlight hung limply in his friend's hand, light pooling around his feet.

The ghost was wearing an old-fashioned white ball gown covered in sparkling crystal beads. Eric remembered Tyler saying something about the dress being given to her by the pirate Durand. She was buried in that dress, he suddenly remembered—and wished he hadn't.

The ghost began to descend the staircase, floating down, rather than taking real steps. She was holding a candelabrum overhead that flickered with *black* flames that seemed to suck light into themselves, making the glowing figure stand out even more.

At first the ghost seemed not to notice the wonderstruck boys. But, when she reached the foot of the stairs, she beckoned for the youngsters to follow.

"She wants us to go with her," Eric said.

"*No way.*" Tyler shook his head emphatically.

The figure gestured again. Her eyes, like two black marbles, seemed to bore into Eric's head. *You must come.* He clearly heard the soft voice in his head, even though the dead lips never moved. It was undoubtedly a command. The boy was sure he could hear an unspoken *Or else* underneath what was said.

"I, um, don't think you want to tick off this ghost," Eric said.

He took a step closer to the phantom. Tyler resisted, until the figure turned her full gaze on him. The cold black eyes locked on his. After a moment, he began to shake from head to toe.

"All right," he said finally. "I'm comin'." He sounded frightened out of his wits. But he took a step forward.

Satisfied, the ghost began to glide down the long hall with the boys in tow. Tyler got control of himself. He began to sweep the flashlight from side to side. Rotting furniture, crumbling drapes, and spiderwebs filled every corner, some even completely covering doorways that opened off the hall. Here and there, they could see marks in the dust coating the floor that probably indicated Rufus had passed by. Whatever dealings Rufus had with the ghost, she hadn't scared him off. Eric began to feel a little better.

Three-quarters of the way down the hall, the figure in glittering white stopped and pointed to a sealed doorway. Eric tried to open it, but it was stuck. Tyler pulled his screwdriver out of his backpack and set to work. In a few minutes, he had freed the ancient lock.

The boys stood on either side as the ghost started down a rickety flight of steps toward what was clearly the basement. She paused only long enough to indicate that the boys were to follow. In the middle of the damp, musty area below, she lingered for a moment, pointing to one wall. Then the figure began slowly fading from view, her arm out-stretched, until she was gone.

"What was *that* all about?" Tyler wondered when he could find his voice.

"I think she was trying to show us something impor-tant. Maybe Mad Dan's treasure."

The wall she had been pointing to was stacked with old trunks and wooden boxes. Their hopes up, the boys eagerly dug through the containers, but they found only dusty, cracked dishes and silverware so tarnished it was solid black; some old hats, dresses, and boots that damp-ness and neglect had reduced to mildewed debris unpleas-ant even to touch; and not much else.

Moving one stack of crates to see what was behind it, Eric discovered an opening, little more than a crack in the wall that a full-grown man might just—barely—edge through if he turned sideways. Borrowing Tyler's flash-light, Eric slipped inside, returned a few minutes later, and reported, "There's a tunnel lined with bricks on the other side of this wall. I'm going to check it out. You don't have to come."

"I'm not staying here by myself," said Tyler decisively.

When they had both squeezed through into the narrow

passage beyond, they began moving cautiously along the tunnel. They followed its twists and turns for a long time, until Tyler said, "We must be real near the water."

A little farther on, they found a deep hole, like a dry well. When Tyler shone his flashlight into the depths, they saw something like metal glimmering. Tyler, his fear apparently forgotten, said, "That's it! We found Mad Daniel Durand's treasure."

"Maybe," said Eric. "But it's down there, and we're up here. I want to check it out."

Tyler's triumphant smile faded. But Eric assured his friend, "Getting down's no problem."

"How? I sure don't see any steps or ladders."

With a smile, Eric pulled out the coil of rope he'd brought, saying, "Help me put some knots in the rope so the climbing is easier." When this was done, they tied the end of the rope securely to a sturdy iron ring—one of several they found embedded along the tunnel wall. Then they lowered the length into the well.

"I'll be okay," said Eric, sounding less sure now that the moment of truth had come. "But if anything happens, you run and get my dad."

Leaving the flashlight with Tyler, Eric turned on his lantern, tying it to his chest with some twine Tyler found in his backpack. Then he began to climb down.

At the bottom he found an oak chest bound with copper bands. These, he guessed, were what had reflected the light earlier. He scraped away the moss and patina that obscured a brass plate affixed to the top of the chest. On it was etched DISTURB THIS NOT, OR THE CURSE OF PYRAT DAN FALL UPON YE.

Eric felt a chill far deeper than the cold damp at the bottom of the well could cause. Did he dare to risk a pirate's curse? But his eagerness to discover what was inside the chest made him think how many times he'd read that people in olden times—Egyptian pharaohs and kings and such—were always using warnings like that to frighten people away. Probably it was only an empty warning.

Probably.

Still, his hands were shaking when he tried to open the chest. But the ancient lock held; the lid refused to budge. He knew he needed Tyler's tools. There was enough rope to loop through the handles at both ends of the chest, so Eric did that. He rocked it carefully, testing the weight, and decided that the two of them, working together, could manage to haul it up. It couldn't be filled with gold or it would be heavier, but Eric imagined there were enough diamonds and rubies to make the boys and their families wealthy for life.

Once the end of the rope was firmly anchored, Eric

shimmied up it, helped by the well-placed knots. The boys began to haul the chest, but when it was halfway up, the rope burst into flames that gave off a stink of burning sulfur. The chest dropped to the bottom of the hole. Leaning into the pit, the boys, to their dismay, saw the chest had cracked in two. A few gold coins and some jewelry had spilled out, but the main contents were horrible. Scattered in the mud were the bones of a man's skeleton—only the skull seemed to be missing. And, issuing like steam from a ruptured pipe, the ghost of Headless Dan swirled up through the gap between the halves of the container. The truncated figure shook its near-transparent fist at them and swiped at the air with a transparent cutlass.

"How can it see us with no head?" asked Tyler.

"I don't know, and I don't *care*! And I'm not staying around to ask," insisted Eric.

"Me neither!" echoed Tyler.

The two charged back along the tunnel toward the basement. They were sure they could hear the sounds of pursuit behind them, spectral boots thudding down the brick-lined passage, the angry sounds of a ghostly cutlass striking the wall with a loud *cling-clang*.

They squeezed through the narrow entrance to the tunnel, not caring how much they scraped hands and arms.

The Haunted Mansion

Then they raced across the basement and back up the stairs to the main floor. There they came to a screeching halt.

The ghost of Emily Summerton was waiting for them in the hall. Her pale form hovered just above the floor, blocking their way to the front door. With a groan, Eric realized that all the doors along the hall that had been open earlier were now firmly shut.

"We can't get out," he said hopelessly, even as he was desperately looking for some way to escape.

Tyler just made a choking sound in his throat,

The words formed in Eric's head: *Give him eternal rest. Then we can be together in eternal peace.* From the expression on Tyler's face, Eric knew his friend had heard the same thing.

Now they could hear the headless horror *clump-clump-clump*ing up the stairs from the cellar.

"How can we help you?" cried Eric, tears of frustration starting from his eyes.

Give him back what he seeks.

Eric was about to ask what she meant, then he guessed. "His head. He has to have his head back."

The ghost nodded once, then vanished. Eric was suddenly aware that the sounds of pursuit had stopped. Both ghosts had gone. The hall doors could now be opened. But when they tried to open the front door or the side doors or any window, they found them sealed fast. Locks wouldn't give; glass wouldn't break; wooden doors had suddenly become as hard and immobile as the steel doors on a bank vault.

"I think we're stuck here until we find the head," Eric said finally. "Otherwise, we might just disappear like you said others have."

Tyler shuddered, but all he said was "It must be hidden somewhere in the house. At least, that's what the old stories say."

"Can you remember anything more from those stories?" asked Eric.

His friend thought for a minute, then said, "There was another story about Ezra Summerton showing the head to his daughter, who fainted away. When she recovered, she asked that he give it to her, to bury properly and give her lover rest. But the old man only laughed at her and said it was hidden where she'd never find it, where he could watch over it day and night, so the ghost would never rest, and his daughter would forever see the error of her ways."

"Nice guy," said Eric bitterly. Then he considered, "If he watched it day and night, it must have been near him when he slept. And didn't you say old Ezra died of fright in his bed? It all makes me think he might have hidden the head in his bedroom."

"Makes sense, I guess," said Tyler, not sounding totally convinced. "We sure got nothing to lose by searching."

They climbed the stairs and started looking into the rooms along the upstairs hall. At the very end, behind fancy double doors, they found what had to be the master bedroom. The huge, heavy wood bedstead, carved all over with angels' and devils' heads, and a bureau were the only pieces of furniture. They peered under the bed and in the empty bureau and behind the dusty drapes and pulled the few rags and odds and ends out of the closet, but found nothing.

Not sure exactly what he was doing, Eric began tapping on the walls and floor, hoping to hear some sort of hollow sound that would indicate a hiding place. But everything seemed solid.

Faint dawn light was beginning to brighten the filthy windows behind the shreds that had once been the finest curtains.

"People will start searchin' for us, soon's they see we're gone," said Tyler, dropping wearily onto the edge of the bed, raising a small cloud of dust. Then he flopped back onto the bed, raising an even bigger cloud.

"I'm not sure how soon they'll think about coming here," said Eric worriedly. "And I'm not so sure what they'll find will be very pretty. We have no food or water. Maybe the ghosts will just get impatient and make us disappear." Then he slammed his right fist into his left palm. "It *has* to be here!"

"We've looked everywhere: under the bed, in the bureau, through the closet. We banged on the walls and floor. There's nowhere you could hide anything as big as a head. There's nothing else in here, 'cept old Ezra's bed."

"Then that's *got* to be the answer," said Eric. He began pounding and slapping at the heavy carved headboard.

"You gone crazy?" asked Tyler, sitting up.

Eric ignored him and just kept poking, prodding, slamming, and running his fingers across the headboard. Suddenly, a portion of the wood slid aside to reveal a secret space. From inside, Eric pulled out a roundish shape, about the size of a football, swathed in grayed linen strips.

"Don't unwrap it," said Tyler. "I am not up to any unwrapping!"

At that instant, the door to the bedroom, which they had closed on entering, burst open. The ghosts—Emily Summerton and Daniel Durand's headless figure—stood framed there. The ghastly pirate leaned upon his cutlass, but Emily was smiling. On an impulse, Eric tossed the linen-wrapped thing to the ghost, which dropped the cutlass and snatched the parcel in midair.

"How's he *do* that with no head?" asked Tyler.

"You're the one who told me not to ask silly questions about how ghosts do what they do," Eric reminded the other boy. There was suddenly a blaze of white light. Daniel Durand, now a whole man again—and smiling—stood beside his lady love. He bowed to the boys; Emily Summerton curtsied.

Then they vanished.

"Not a bad night's work," said Eric, when his amazement at the recent events had eased a little. "We helped a couple of ghosts find rest, and we found at least a part of the pirate's treasure."

"Oh, yeah," Tyler said. "I almost forgot what's down in the well." Then he paused. "Do you think the ghosts will let us take that stuff?"

"I think they're mixed up in much more important stuff now. I don't think they'll ever come back," Eric assured his friend.

"I guess we can't tell their story to anyone," said Eric thoughtfully. "I mean, who's going to believe our ghost story?"

"It's too good a story not to tell—*sometime*," said Tyler. "But only when the time is right. And the gold and jewels will be proof that we aren't lying."

"That's right," Eric agreed as they started downstairs. They paused to open the front door on another sunny Findings Island morning. The storm had blown over, and the gentle breeze wafting in was fresh with promise. It was a very good day indeed.

Go Fish!

GO FISH

ROBERT D. SAN SOUCI

What did you want to be when you grew up?
As far back as I can remember, I always wanted to be a writer. I grew up in a family that treasured books and writers—for the enjoyment they provided, for the information they imparted, and for the sheer love of good stories and good writing.

Were you a reader or a non-reader growing up?
I was an inveterate reader from the time I learned to read. Before that, according to reports, I would pretend to read my picture books by pointing to the illustrations and reconstructing the story as best I could from the memory of having someone read it to me.

When did you realize you wanted to be a writer?
Pretty much all my life. I was trying to sell stories to publishers by the time I was in second grade. I would get the name and address of an editor (with the help of my local librarian, who was always encouraging me) and use my weekly allowance to pay the postage. Of course, none of those early efforts sold—but I was never discouraged, sending story after story to editor after editor year after year. I felt I was destined to be published; it just wound up taking a lot longer than I'd hoped!

What's your most embarrassing childhood memory?

In fifth grade, for our class holiday program, I wrote what I thought was a hilarious skit about a naughty little boy whom Santa Claus visits on Christmas night. At the time I was a huge fan of Three Stooges slapstick comedies on TV (what can I say: I still get a giggle from the Stooges' antics). I thought there was nothing funnier than a pie in the face. My skit was supposed to end with the naughty little boy, played by my best friend, John, hitting Santa (myself) in the face with a "pie" (what was supposed to be a soft cardboard pie form filled with shaving cream). I didn't know that John had lost the cardboard shell, and substituted one of his mother's tin baking dishes. At the playlet's climactic moment, in front of the fifth grade class and our increasingly nervous teacher, Sister Rosemarie (this was a Catholic school), he slammed the metal pie plate into my face, nearly (not quite) breaking my nose. Stunned by the pain, and blinded by the shaving cream, which burned my eyes, I sensed my nose begin to bleed. (It wasn't until later that I found out the shaving cream had splattered Sister and several students.) In agony, I stumbled toward the door; I wanted only to find the boys' bathroom and put a wet, cold towel on my aching nose. In the hall I blundered into Sister Hilary, the school principal, who was coming to find out what all the yelling was for. I left her nun's robe smeared with blood and shaving cream as I bumbled down the hall in search of a cold compress. Needless to say, that was the end of my playwriting career for several years.

What's your favorite childhood memory?

I think listening to my grandfather and uncle on my mother's side of the family, who were of Irish extraction and great storytellers, tell the timeless tales of heroes, leprechauns, pookas, banshees, and so forth. I think this had a lot of influence on my love of both writing and telling stories.

As a young person, who did you look up to most?
I admired the writers of scary stories, fantasy, science fiction, and adventure tales who could, at times, create whole worlds to fill the imagination, people them with characters I wished I could meet, and hold an audience spellbound with the magic of words.

What was your favorite thing about school?
English classes, writing exercises, and, occasionally, having the teacher read aloud to the class.

What was your least favorite thing about school?
I liked sports, but I was not very good at baseball, football, or whatever. When teams were picked, I was always the last to be chosen. And often there would be the dreaded phrase: "We'll take San Souci, but only if we get to choose someone *good* at the same time."

What were your hobbies as a kid? What are your hobbies now?
I was always visiting used bookstores, spending allowance money and the money from odd jobs to collect books. As a child, I also loved building plastic models from kits—especially rocket ships, flying saucers, anything with a science fiction element. Nowadays, I still collect books. I also love to travel; I make a point to visit museums, libraries, historical societies, etc.—and take any "haunted house" tours an area might offer—in order to learn all I can about a place. Much that I've learned has found its way into stories one way or another.

What was your first job, and what was your "worst" job?
My first job was mowing lawns on Saturdays in my neighborhood for fifty cents an hour. My worst job, years ago, was taking care of some friends' pets while they were on vacation. The cat was sick and had to take pills and would fight and claw and bite and spit out the pills and hide from me. The puppy wasn't housebroken and would make mess after mess in the living room or dining room. It would get into the bathroom, grab the toilet paper, then drag it all over the house and shred it. The house looked like a snowstorm had hit it. The worst, no question.

What book is on your nightstand now?
The Random House Book of Ghost Stories, edited by Susan Hill. I'd read this collection years ago, but I'm enjoying getting reacquainted with the ghosts and some of the haunted houses they inhabit.

How did you celebrate publishing your first book?
My first book, *The Legend of Scarface*, a retelling of a Blackfeet Lodge tale, was illustrated by my brother, Daniel. When it was published, we took our family out to dinner to celebrate the launching of our careers.

Where do you write your books?
I do the bulk of my writing in my office in my house in San Francisco, working at the computer. But, as much as I can, I like to work on my stories or novels at a local coffeehouse or (if the weather is good) park, just to get a change of scenery and enjoy a little sunshine and fresh air.

What sparked your imagination for *Haunted Houses*?

I've always loved scary stories in general, but tales of haunted houses—either fictional or reportedly true accounts of actual hauntings—have been a lifelong fascination for me. I've done a number of story collections in which I have included a haunted house tale. But the idea of a book devoted only to haunted houses intrigued me. To allow for a variety of tales and moods, I set stories in a haunted doll house, a dog house, a Japanese tea house, and so on. It was fun to discover just how many ways I could take the idea of a haunted house (or wherever) and manage to keep the storytelling fresh and vital.

What challenges do you face in the writing process, and how do you overcome them?

The hardest thing for me (and, I think, for many writers) is to keep the importance of rewriting always in mind. Sometimes I'm tempted to say, This story's done, when I know it needs a bit more tweaking. I overcome the tendency to let a not-quite-finished story go to market by reminding myself that the effort is only going to improve the final result—and make it more appealing to an editor.

Which of your characters is most like you?

That's hard to say. I think many of my characters remind me of me in one way or another. In *Haunted Houses*, I might compare myself to Larry Hamada in "Tea House." He's bright, intelligent, driven by curiosity about both the seen and unseen worlds. But he's also cautious, not wanting to push things too far too fast. He contrasts with Kat, who's a bit on the reckless side, though she's brave and intelligent and loyal. They make a good team: Larry erring on the side of caution; Kat on the side of "Let's push the envelope and deal with consequences later." Yes, I'm decidedly more Larry than Kat.

What makes you laugh out loud?
Funny writing in any form. I love funny writing from the classic "Canterville Ghost" of Oscar Wilde to the comic fantasies of Terry Pratchett set in the Discworld universe, with its silly witches, goofy wizards, and amusing monsters of every sort. Nothing is more satisfying to me than to laugh aloud, even though it may sometimes make people look at you, then look at you again, then move away slightly.

What do you do on a rainy day?
If I'm not actually writing, I find the atmosphere is perfect for curling up with a good scary story or DVD.

What's your idea of fun?
Relaxing with friends, sharing stories, just enjoying good company—especially if there are some first-rate storytellers in the bunch.

What's your favorite song?
I have two, both oldies: "Laura" is the theme song from the movie of the same title about a mysterious woman—perhaps dead, perhaps not—who haunts the hero of the film. The other is "Stella by Starlight," the theme from one of my all-time favorite ghost films, *The Uninvited*, about a young woman tormented by a ghost (or are there two?) from her past. Favorite songs that conjure up favorite movies.

Who is your favorite fictional character?

My first favorite character was Dorothy Gale in *The Wizard of Oz*, book and movie. When I was older, I admired John Carter of Mars in the series of books by Edgar Rice Burroughs, who also wrote the Tarzan series. I read so much and so widely, it's hard to pick a single character. One of my favorites is certainly Percy Jackson in Rick Riordan's Percy Jackson and the Olympians series, updating Greek mythology in a contemporary setting.

What was your favorite book when you were a kid? Do you have a favorite book now?

As already mentioned, *The Wizard of Oz* by L. Frank Baum was a standout favorite—one of the first books I was given, and one I value to this day. *The Haunting of Hill House* by Shirley Jackson, a novel I discovered in high school, is probably my all-time favorite adult book. She can turn a phrase or create an image that sticks in my mind even after I've read it almost twenty times.

What's your favorite TV show or movie?

Far and away, the *X Files* was, and remains, my favorite TV show. I love watching and rewatching such classic scary movies as the Alien series, *Poltergeist*, *The Sixth Sense*, *The Exorcist*, and even the funny *Ghostbusters*.

If you were stranded on a desert island, who would you want for company?

Another writer who works in the scary stories genre like myself. I can imagine great conversations with writers like Shirley Jackson, Stephen King, R. L. Stine, Clive Barker, Dean Koontz—the list could go on forever.

If you could travel anywhere in the world, where would you go and what would you do?

I'd love to spend time in Egypt, exploring the pyramids, temple ruins, and so on.

If you could travel in time, where would you go and what would you do?

I'd project myself into the future, hopefully find a world where interstellar travel was a reality, visit an infinite variety of star systems and planets, and encounter all kinds of strange beings and civilizations.

What's the best advice you have ever received about writing?

Have faith in yourself and what you're attempting as a writer. Don't give up. Just because ten editors are unresponsive to what you've created doesn't mean there isn't an eleventh who will "get" you and your creations.

What advice do you wish someone had given you when you were younger?

Don't worry if someone—a critic or whoever—doesn't like or appreciate your writing. Don't be overly sensitive to negative input. Keep the faith. Such advice would have made it easier for me as a beginning writer not to stew about a bad review or negative feedback, and to realize that you're never going to please everyone all the time.

Do you ever get writer's block? What do you do to get back on track?

I rarely get writer's block. My problem is that I'm constantly getting ideas for stories from things I see, people I meet, places I visit, and accounts that I hear or read. My challenge is to pick the best of the lot and keep focus. Trying to follow too many story threads leads me to a point where a lot is started but not a lot gets completed. It's not writer's block, but the writer can get stymied if he or she becomes pulled in too many directions at once. Focus is the key. I keep reminding myself: stay focused.

What do you want readers to remember about your books?

Hopefully, that the story or book provided them great entertainment, maybe an idea or two, and embodied good writing with interesting characters and an intriguing plotline—enough that they'll want to come back for a second read, recommend the book to friends, and look forward to my next creation.

What would you do if you ever stopped writing?

I'd still do something that kept me in touch with books and writing on some level. I'd work as an editor helping other writers to publication, perhaps sell books, or maybe try to establish myself as a book reviewer.

What should people know about you?

I like people. I'm easy to approach, to talk to, to get to know. If they're interested in me, they'll find I'm equally interested in them.

What do you like best about yourself?

That I'm a "people person," always interested in meeting new folks and hearing their stories (we all have stories to share). I rarely find anyone with whom I can't feel comfortable.

Do you have any strange or funny habits? Did you when you were a kid?

I never go anywhere without a book. Even a trip to the grocery store means tucking a book into my backpack, since you never know when a quiet moment will present itself. I'm sort of obsessed with books and reading. When I was very young and my brother, Daniel, the artist, was younger, he told our mother, in all seriousness, that he was worried that "Bob is always reading, reading, reading. I think he's going to read too much and burn out his brain." Fortunately, that hasn't happened (so far).

What do you consider to be your greatest accomplishment?

I'd have to say it's the publication of over 100 books and the fulfillment of my childhood dreams.

What do you wish you could do better?

I truly believe there's plenty of room for improving my writing. I constantly try to improve myself during the writing process, learning from better writers about how they approach the creation of stories and books. I always hope that my next book will be my best.

What would your readers be most surprised to learn about you?

Many readers who come to me through my scary story collections are surprised to learn that I write numerous picture books for younger and very young readers: retellings of folktales and fairytales, humorous stories, romantic "happily ever after" tales—stories with no scary edge whatsoever.

Read the Allie Nichols Ghost Mysteries
AVAILABLE FROM SQUARE FISH

The Ghost of Fossil Glen • 978-0-312-60213-0

A murdered girl is sending messages to Allie,
asking to have her death avenged.
Is Allie brave enough to confront a killer?

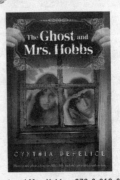

The Ghost and Mrs. Hobbs • 978-0-312-62909-0

Allie is being haunted by a handsome
young man who needs her help dealing with
a dangerous person. Or is he the dangerous one?

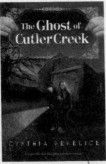

The Ghost of Cutler Creek • 978-0-312-62967-0

Another ghost is trying to contact Allie,
but how can she help a ghost who won't speak?
Is it possible this ghost was never human?

The Ghost of Poplar Point • 978-0-374-32540-4

A ghost is haunting Allie's dreams with
frightening scenes. But if Allie tries to
help this ghost, she could risk destroying
her entire town.

Six chilling tales

AVAILABLE FROM SQUARE FISH

The Adoration of Jenna Fox
Mary E. Pearson
ISBN: 978-0-312-59441-1
$8.99 US / $11.50 Can

What happened to Jenna Fox?
And who is she, really?

The Compound
S.A. Bodeen
ISBN: 978-0-312-57860-2
$8.99 US / $11.50 Can

Eli's father built the Compound to
keep his family safe. But are they
safe—or sorry?

Dead Connection
Charlie Price
ISBN: 978-0-312-37966-7
$7.99 US / $10.25 Can

Can Murray's ability to talk
to dead people help him find
a missing cheerleader?

Holdup
Terri Fields
ISBN: 978-0-312-56130-7
$8.99 US / $11.50 Can

The most dangerous thing at Burger
Heaven should be greasy food,
not a maniac with a gun.

The Love Curse of the Rumbaughs
Jack Gantos
ISBN: 978-0-312-38052-6
$7.99 US / $8.99 Can

Ivy has two great loves, her mother
and taxidermy.

Zombie Blondes
Brian James
ISBN: 978-0-312-57375-1
$8.99 US / $11.50 Can

All of the girls in Hannah's
new school are blonde and
popular—and dead.